How to Love

Jazmin Billings
A Life Better Than Yours Doesn't Exist

Dedication

"To every little girl inside every woman who has ever thought she was wasn't enough....a life better than yours doesn't exist!"

Acknowledgment

I want to thank everyone who inspired me to put my ideas into words. Your encouragement and support paved the way for my creativity.

About the Author

Active imagination, creative accuracy, and a hint of social awareness, Jazmin Billings is a complete package as a fiction author. Her debut novel How To Love is a testament to her amazing ability to pull the reader into a world of her own.

Born and raised in a southern, rural town, known for its agriculture and athletes, Jazmin found refuge at the age of eight in another African American woman, Janice Abbott.

Janice Abbott challenged Jazmin to always be more, no matter what more entailed. As an Army Veteran, Jazmin is giving the world more through her writing by inspiring young African American women that they too are more.

Contents

Page Left Blank Intentionally

Chapter 1

"NICOLE TAYLOR!" the assistant principal announced – the same who had called out Nicole's older sister Jade's name at the time of her graduation. The tone, the pitch, even the atmosphere was identical – well, almost, except for one small detail: their mother wasn't present for Jade's graduation. She had only arrived two hours late high on one of the many prescription drugs she was abusing.

Despite, or perhaps even because of, the horrendous memory of the same room from four years ago, Jade was very proud of her little sister. No one had expected Nicole to graduate. She was the type of student who attended school three out of five days a week and even then only to make a fashion statement.

She was not very studious, but her beauty and hourglass-shaped body made up for all the other things she lacked. Jade and their mother, Michelle, waited in the parking lot to greet Nicole after the ceremony. From the looks of it, no one could tell every time they were together; it was a disaster. The reason for their estranged relationship started long ago – precisely the time that Jade's father married another woman while Michelle was pregnant with her. He tried being a dad to Jade for a while, but eventually, his part-time father act faded, and he became one of those complete absent fathers. All of this happened before Jade was even two years old.

Michelle hated the man so much she started to direct her spite towards Jade when he no longer came around. Things never got better from thereon. Despite the strained relationship between mother and daughter, the two pretended to like each other for Nicole's big day.

"Is there a particular reason you chose that color dress?" Michelle said, her eyes roving up and down her daughter's clothes.

Jade followed the movement of her eyes, and unconsciously ran her hand down the front of her dress then silently cursed for showing how much her mother's casual remarks got to her. "Yellow is my favorite color; you know that," she answered.

"Honey, your complexion is far too dark for bright colors. You know what's more your style?"

Jade didn't answer, but her mother informed her anyway: "Earth tone colors. Try wearing those."

Jade opened her mouth to respond, but just then, Nicole and a group of her friends walked towards them, stopping the conversation before it took a turn for the worse.

"Jade, sweetie you can take the photos," Michelle handed the camera to Jade as Nicole approached.

Jade snapped a few pictures as Michelle wrapped her arms around Nicole, and the two of them smiled for the camera.

"Come on, pile up in the car. We're gonna get something to eat," Michelle said.

It was a celebration dinner. The family was far from perfect but never failed to put up a good face in public.

Midway through the meal, Michelle made a toast to her daughter's accomplishment.

"I remember the exact day you were born – a special moment just as precious as this one. This is just the beginning, only the first of the many accomplishments which lie ahead of you. I can't wait to see your beautiful face and perfect skin on the big screen in Hollywood. I love you, Red."

Nicole giggled and couldn't hide the red blotches showing through her fair skin. She felt like the only person in the world. Michelle raised her glass and glanced at Jade from the corner of her eye. Jade pretended to not notice. This moment triggered the memories of so many other similar incidents in Jade's memory. She had grown accustomed to her mom's favoritism for Nicole.

She never showed she cared, though, and always masked her true feelings even as she boiled with hurt and hatred on the inside. Since she was a child, Jade had imagined herself exploding with emotions. She could just picture herself erupting one day, like Mount Vesuvius; she'd seen its pictures in her textbook. She wanted to tell Michelle exactly how she felt. "How could you have two daughters and only acknowledge one? I am the better daughter anyways. But you live in your little fairytale bubble and pretend that I don't exist until your lights are due, and you're hungry."

She seethed with anger, but she played nice. She didn't exactly know why she continued being nice and polite to her mom when what she really wanted was to break things and show her she wasn't someone to be taken lightly. After dinner, Michelle went home. Jade took Nicole back to her apartment as she had a big night planned for her. Nicole's favorite artist was performing in town, and Jade was lucky enough to score front row tickets and backstage passes.

"Tonight is a night you will never forget. I already have our tickets, pregame bottles, and little black dresses back at my apartment. You don't have to worry about a thing, just let go and have fun."

Nicole laughed, intending to do just that.

Jade and Nicole stood in a long line to get into the venue. A man wearing a shirt that said "Security" was walking past them, and Nicole got his attention.

"Excuse me, sir, do I have to stand in this ridiculously long line if I have a backstage pass?"

The man looked at Nicole as she batted her synthetic eyelashes at him. "Nah, baby girl," the man smiled and showed his gold teeth. "Follow me; I can get you in."

The girls walked past the long line of people. They could feel the jealousy from all the females, and the men were practically throwing themselves at them. Nicole was used to this kind of attention – she was practically reveling in it – but Jade felt uncomfortable by all the envy being directed their way. They finally reached the front of the line. Jade tried to give the bouncer the backstage passes she had bought three weeks ago. He never acknowledged her; his eyes were fixed on Nicole. She was beautiful. Her perfect skin and sparkling eyes matched her curvaceous body and flirtatious charisma. The bouncer unhooked the rope and didn't bother taking the tickets from Jade. "Upstairs to the left, beautiful," he said, his gaze flitting from Nicole's body to her face then back again.

"Don't break too many hearts tonight, sis," Jade whispered, and Nicole chuckled deep from her throat in response.

About four drinks, six shots, and two marijuana joints later, there was no more party in either of the girls. Jade was drunk, and Nicole was high. Neither of them was in any condition to drive. A guy leaving the club as they swayed on the sidewalk noticed them. Jade stumbled to the driver's side of the car, and Nicole laughed hysterically every time she lost her footing. As soon as Jade opened the door, the guy rushed to her. He put his hands on hers and looked into her eyes.

"You don't want to do that, little lady." Panting with sincerity, he added, "Allow me."

Barely able to open her eyes, Jade poked him in the chest, "Do I know you?"

"I may have seen you around campus if that counts for anything."

"Let me see your driver's license and school ID, and I may consider allowing you to drive us home," Jade said between hiccups.

The man pulled out his wallet and handed it to Jade.

"Mr. Devin Watson from Savannah, Georgia, a third-year student at Tech." Her words were slurred, her eyes shining and her face too bright. "If I am sober enough to read this small ass writing, then I am sober enough to drive home." She pushed past the guy and plopped on the driver's seat, stretching her legs and shaking her head in a futile attempt to clear away the cobwebs of confusion.

Police lights glared at her through the rearview mirror as Jade sat in the driver's seat.

"Everything okay here, folks?" a stern yet concerned voice

blared over the loudspeaker.

"Yes, sir," Devin responded. "The ladies had a few drinks, and I was just about to drive them home."

"Alright, now make sure you do that," the loudspeaker yelled back, and the police car drove away.

"Now, may I please make sure you get home safely?"

She got out of the car and climbed into the backseat but not before giving the accidental rescue guy a long stare. The streetlights danced in front of her eyes, and when she closed her tired eyelids for a few seconds, bright specks illuminated the darkness.

The next morning, Jade woke up in her own bed. Her mouth felt as dry as cotton, and her head seemed to weigh a ton. She was more in her senses now than the night before, however, and knew enough to wonder how she had got into bed. She didn't remember walking inside her apartment; for that matter, she didn't even remember getting out of the car. Closing her eyes, she thought hard about it: the last thing she recalled was the lights skipping and hopping, like dazzling fireworks, behind her closed lids. Yawning, she rolled her neck only to wince from pain even at that slight movement.

Gingerly, she slid off the bed until her bare feet hit the cold floor, giving her a much-needed shock. Her head was pounding, and she could feel her temporal vein pulsing. She stumbled her way to the kitchen and found Nicole flipping pancakes. The smell from the cooking made her want to throw up.

"Good morning, big sis. How did you sleep?" Nicole asked, grinning at her sister's disheveled state. Jade did look funny. There were mascara smears underneath her eyes, and her hair stuck out in tufts.

Jade groaned and sat down in the middle of the floor. She looked around, bewildered. When she spoke, it became apparent she'd had a case of temporary amnesia. "What happened last night?"

"Are you serious right now?"

"I don't remember anything."

"Well, I remember e-ver-y-thing," Nicole said with a smirk on her face. "So, you don't remember Devin?"

"Devin, who?"

"Devin Watson!"

"Nah, the name doesn't ring a bell."

"Well," Nicole smirked. "He definitely knows who you are."

She wriggled her eyebrows at Jade until Jade said, "Great. I slept with him and don't remember."

It was nothing new for Jade. She had a track record for one-night stands during times she was near blackout drunk. She had slept with guys she barely knew. Even so, she buried her face into her hands.

"You didn't sleep with him; he didn't even come into the apartment. He walked us to the door and left," Nicole reassured her, finally taking pity on her sister's state.

"How did he look?"

"Just how you like them! Light skin, neat dreads, and clean cut. It looked like he works out too. I'm not sure though; I was high as hell last night."

"That's beside the point," Nicole insisted. "Let me tell you about what I'm about to be doing." Jade heard Nicole, but she wasn't listening. She was still trying to remember what had happened the night before. Nicole continued to ramble, but her voice faded into the background for Jade. The only thing on her mind was Devin. Although they had never really "met," she was already into him, simply because they did not have sex. Jade was accustomed to waking up the morning after a drunken night filled with regret from unconscious sex with a stranger from the night before.

"Jade, do you think I should take four or five classes in my first semester while working part-time?" Nicole shouted because she knew she was being ignored.

"Huh?" Jade responded. "Oh, I'm sorry. Yeah, you have to manage your time well."

"I figure I can pocket the financial aid money for at least two semesters and work a full-time job to have enough money saved to move to Los Angeles," Nicole added.

Nicole had it all figured out, while Jade was in a daze trying to piece together events from a night ago. Nicole had been waiting for the day she could graduate and prove she was independent. This was her chance, and she was ready. Jade, on the other hand, was stunned by the thought of Devin Watson, all she knew was that she had to meet him, no matter what it.

Chapter 2

"Pass the joint, Nic," a raspy voice demanded. "I know you nervous, baby girl, but you can't be stingy with the loud."

Nicole took another long hit before passing the cocaine-laced, marijuana joint to her best friend, Rachel. She held it in a couple of seconds longer than usual before slowly exhaling.

"Yeah, that's right!" Rachel shouted from across the dressing room filled with half-naked girls waiting to get high as well.

Nicole was sitting on a barstool, holding her head down. She could feel the room spinning as she slowly sat up, looking at herself in the lightbulb-bordered mirror. She stared into her own eyes through the mirror.

No longer was she the high school graduate with big movie star dreams. Now, she was a community college dropout and a drug-addicted stripper. This was her first night performing at Cloey's, and she was nowhere near ready. She picked up the black pencil to begin applying eyeliner to her face. Rachel came over, and through the vibration of the steel lockers from the loudspeaker, the thick clouds of marijuana smoke, and the stench of sweat and vomit, whispered in her ear. "Here, take this shot."

Nicole turned around and looked her best friend right in the eyes, although her own eyes were barely open.

"Don't worry about a thing," she said, "just let go, and the rest will happen. It's on." Nicole tossed the vodka down the back of her throat. The alcohol sent a burning sensation to her esophagus down to her stomach, resulting in chills throughout her body.

"Now, finish getting dressed - it's almost happy hour!"

Her hair was already done from earlier that day, in big, bouncy, waterfall curls. She rubbed baby oil all over her perfect porcelain skin, so instead of sweating, she would just glisten.

She borrowed a pair of Rachel's four-inch black pumps with the red bottom to match her debut outfit: a pair of black, lace boy shorts and a black transparent silk robe with red fur trim. She accessorized it with the red, horned hair clip, to reflect the illusion of the devil's wife.

Finally, getting the outfit to perfectly expose her curves, she looked in a full-length mirror one last time, trying to convince herself somehow that what she was doing was justified. She remembered her mom preparing her for her first date with an older man, hearing her voice in her head: "Sometimes you have to use what you have to get what you want."

Then she thought of her sister Jade and how she seemed to always have herself together. At that very moment, she wished she was Jade. Nicole wished she was smart and made good grades in high school to earn a scholarship, as Jade had. She wished she was strong enough to make a respectable income instead of showing her body to complete strangers.

As the feeling of self-pity started to consume her, the vodka she had taken earlier hit her all at once. She became dizzy, and her head started to spin. She stumbled to the chair, and Rachel gave her a glass of water.

"Drink this," she said urgently. "You're going on in two minutes."

Nicole swallowed three big gulps. She gargled the fourth and spit it on the floor. She could hear Ms. Foxy on the microphone introducing her, so she walked to the closest position backstage so she'd be right in the spotlight as soon as the curtains opened. Her palms began to sweat, and her heart felt like it was about to jump out of her chest.

"If you're broke, then don't even bother. She is all about the money, so she ain't scared of the pole. Now get them dollars out and show my girl some love - the promiscuous, the sexy, the beautiful Ms. Candi!"

The curtain slowly opened, revealing to the club what they had been waiting for. Shy, nervous, embarrassed, and yet excited at the same time, Nicole cat-walked down the stage to the stripper pole. She had the full attention of every penis within view. The guys nearest the stage were practically trying to grab her.

As she got within arms-length of the pole, a fair-skinned, wavy-haired man with gold teeth touched her leg, attempting to caress it with a crisp $20 bill. Startled, she snapped her foot back briskly, throwing herself off balance in the four-inch heels. Luckily, right before landing face-first on the platform, she caught herself with the aid of the pole. At the same time, her rear end was straight up in the air, and her face was looking at the spectators upside down, between her legs. Not even realizing she'd had a close call, every guy in the club was on his feet with an erection and throwing money at her. She tried not to focus on the bills at her feet, but on getting through her segment of the show. She slowly began to lift her head upright, arching her lower back while squatting all at the same time. This only aroused the club even more.

Every guy in the audience could tell it was Nicole's first dance, but that made it even more appealing to them. Unlike the other dancers, Nicole was the full package. She had a beautiful face and a perfect physique. After her two-song rotation, Nicole collected all her earnings in a clear garbage bag before going back to the locker room.

She was on cloud nine as she left the stage. She sat on the bench and threw the garbage bag full of money in a locker. She sat there in a daze, partially proud but disgusted as well. Finally, she reached into the locker, pulling out a handful of money and organizing all the bills from biggest to smallest. On her last handful, Rachel stormed into the locker room, looking more excited than ever.

"Girl, you work that crowd like none other."

Nicole looked at her nonchalantly, not knowing whether to sulk or celebrate.

"Now, come on! Let's go get some more."

Nicole hesitated before actually moving. She was skeptical about going into the crowd and giving private dances as opposed to pole dancing on stage. Rachel had already informed her she would make more money doing private dances. She still couldn't understand how, as she admired the pile of money she had made by doing pole dances.

She glanced at the clock and noticed it was only a quarter past ten. She looked back at Rachel as she raised her eyebrows and mischievously stated, "The night is still young. Barbecue or mildew?"

Nicole took a deep breath and replied, "Let's get this money...after another shot."

She walked over to the counter and picked up the bottle of Vodka. Without even bothering to pour it in a shot glass, she drank the alcohol right from the bottle. She sat it down hard on the counter and began to prance out the door, up the four steps and into the club.

The scene from this view was a lot different from being on stage. Nicole felt as though all the attention wasn't on her, almost like she was blending in with everyone else. But as much as she didn't want to stand out, she did. Before she could even walk a few steps into the club, an older man with salt and pepper hair pulled her arm, waving fifteen dollars with his other hand. She didn't hesitate.

She straddled him and began to move her hips to the beat of the song. Although she was face to face with the guy, she was not looking at him but looking past him. Her mother had taught her to not get attached to the moment by avoiding eye contact. She leaned forward to make sure her breast made contact with his face. At this point, she was more focused on making money than how she was getting it.

Her mind was in a totally different place. She snapped back into reality when Rachel held up two fingers, reminding her a private dance was for only two songs. As the song was fading into another, she quickly got up and was immediately grabbed by another interested fellow. This went on for about six guys straight. It was as if the guys were in line, waiting for her to be vacant. Nicole had just successfully entertained for six private dances, and she had a lot of money, so she headed to the locker room. She pulled the money off herself and started to count. Before she was done, she asked one of the other girls in the locker room, "Hey, what's fifteen times six?"

The girl paused for a second as she did the math then blurted out, "$90."

But Nicole had counted $110, so someone had given her an extra twenty dollars.

Now she was more confident, ready for round two. This time, she wasn't as nervous as she climbed up the stairs. She was calm and focused. She had reached the club, but this time around, she was on a mission. Midway through the room, she had rejected three guys flashing money. She wanted to feel in charge, so she thought she could choose whom she would give a private dance to.

That was the type of attitude and confidence Nicole normally carried as if she could have her way by any means necessary. Although this was her first night performing, she was already in love with the fast money and the attention that came with it. As she floated through the club, turning guys down one after the other, she set eyes on an attractive young man across the room. She walked up to him and without saying a word, she sat him in a chair and began to grind on him. Unlike her previous private dances, she was level-headed now, and it was more of an art than a job. Nicole felt the bulge in his pants and began to move more passionately. The song ended, and the man whispered in her ear, "What's your name?" She looked back at him and walked away.

Nicole was notorious for the illusion of sincerity. She had the reputation of a seducer. But she needed that last dance to please her ego. She earned $472 on her debut night and a clientele that would support her goddess-like body. The money she made at Cloey's was a two-week paycheck at the supermarket. Becoming a stripper had never been a goal, but at the end of the day, she had her dignity. Besides the ego boost, the money was all that mattered to her.

She could feel the tension in the air from the rest of the girls in the dressing room. She didn't pay them any attention and left the building to wait by the car instead. As she was walking out of the building, a man ran behind her.

"Hey, beautiful. Wait up!" he said.

"I'm off," replied Nicole, "leave me alone," She was terrified when he started to follow her and started to walk faster to keep distance between them.

"Slow down! I just want to talk to you for a second," he said.

She usually kept pepper spray in her purse. At the moment she needed it the most, she couldn't find it. Luckily, she had grabbed the keys to Rachel's car as she was leaving, but it wasn't long after until Rachel was at the car as well, and the girls headed home.

The next morning Nicole woke up and laid in bed, staring at the ceiling. She thought about how high school was so much fun with no worries. She never imagined it would be so complicated to be an adult. She had witnessed Jade moving out on her own and going to college. She wanted to be like Jade, independent, smart, and determined. She often hated herself because she always compared herself to Jade. Her phone vibrated on the pillow next to her head. It was Jade.

"Track meet at 1:30, wanna go?"

Nicole replied, "Sure, I'll meet you there." It was already eleven, so Nicole managed to get herself out of bed and get dressed to catch the midday bus.

Chapter 3

On the way to Jade, Nicole contemplated whether or not she should tell her about the new job. After slight consideration, she decided it wasn't the right time.

"Hey, it seems like forever since I've seen you!" said Jade. She was right. The sisters had not seen each other since the day after Nicole's graduation. Although they kept in touch, they still felt like they had a lot of catching up to do.

"So how have you been, Nic? How's work and school, of course?" Jade asked. "And I want to know everything."

Nicole felt her insides grind when Jade mentioned school. She didn't want her to know she hadn't been in a whole month, and she most definitely didn't want her to know she quit the supermarket to become a stripper. She had no other option but to simply tell Jade exactly what she wanted to hear.

"Well, you already know I've never been a big fan of school and work is just work."

Jade smiled. "See, I knew you'd make it happen. Once you start doing it, it becomes second nature."

Once Nicole saw Jade bought the lie, she amped it up, so there was no doubt in Jade's mind about what she was doing. "At first, I had a hard time working the cash register, but now it's easy like Sunday morning."

Jade fell victim to every word Nicole spoke. But then, she has always been naïve. Her own honesty was her worst enemy. Because she was so honest, she presumed everyone else was as morally equal. Even her own family would deceive her and take advantage of her innocence.

Nicole felt guilty about lying to her sister, but not enough to feel remorse. She knew if she told Jade the truth, there would be no way to justify it. Maybe the part about becoming a stripper, but not about dropping out of school. Nicole decided she would eventually tell her the truth one day, but today was not that day.

The girls pulled up to the college stadium, and Jade asked, "Do you want to sit in the bleachers or be on the field with me?"

"Of course, I want to be on the field, duh!"

"OK. Well, I have to run to the training room first."

Jade was the senior student physical trainer, which

essentially meant she was already an athletic trainer despite not being certified yet. She supervised five underclassmen. In fact, she knew her job so well and did it so efficiently; the trainer on payroll didn't have to do anything but show up at the sporting event.

Jade was in her last semester and already had three major job offers. She had not told anyone, especially not Nicole, because the offers were all out of state.

Inside the training room were all the sprinters, male and female, with heating pads being stretched. Tech University was hosting its annual "Elite Relays," and Jade was as excited as all the athletes.

Nicole wasn't really a sports fan, but she enjoyed seeing Jade work. Jade grabbed her extra training bag, and the girls made their way through the locker room and onto the field. The field events were still going on, and it would be at least another hour before the track events would begin.

On the field, Jade was at home. Anywhere there were athletes, Jade was happy. She had a passion for what she did, and she was very good at it. All the athletes at Tech knew her by name and made it their business to acknowledge her whenever they saw her around campus.

Jade began to gain national recognition in her sophomore year after she rehabilitated Tech's basketball star, Elijah Combs. Combs was a senior and tore his meniscus tendon early in the season. If Tech had a chance to make a run at the National Championship, they would need a healthy Combs. Jade worked with Combs relentlessly throughout the season, and he was back at 100% a week before the tournament. Doctors and other medical professionals called it a miracle. No one had seen so expedient of a recovery.

Although the athletes knew her for great work in sports, she unfortunately also had a reputation for her bedroom activities. She was known for partying hard and get laid afterward. But she never let her personal lifestyle interfere with her work.

Nicole hung out on the bench with the rest of the trainers from Tech and the other schools, while Jade walked along the long jump sand pit to make sure the Tech athletes were ready to perform. While doing her rounds, she noticed a guy from across the field, staring at her. He watched her talk to each of her athletes. She smiled and tried to pretend like she didn't notice him, but he knew that she knew he was staring.

She was curious to know who this guy was but didn't want to appear desperate. All she could make out was he was wearing a "Tech University Athletics" tee-shirt.

She made her way back to the trainers' area where the paramedics were staged as well. There was an ambulance at every sporting event held at Tech, and Jade knew all the paramedics by name. She'd had a short-lived fling with the ambulance driver. Jade wasn't surprised when it didn't develop into a relationship; she was used to that kind of treatment. To ease her conscience and make herself feel better, she would tell herself, "It wasn't meant to be anyways."

Jade always made it her business to greet the paramedics, somewhat out of respect for the business, and also to see the sick look on his face. Because she was so used to being turned down and taken advantage of, she could talk to him like nothing ever happened. He couldn't even look at her. He would always appear to be busy to avoid eye contact. Jade was amused by the awkward moments.

There were about 30 minutes before the first heat of the female sprints. Nicole watched her sister walk back and forth across the field, and she couldn't have been more proud. The few times she witnessed Jade in action, she had loved seeing her sister happy. After all the checking up on things and reassurances, Jade stood by until she was needed.

"When I was over by the long jumpers, some guy was staring at me something fierce," Jade told Nicole.

"Really? Who was he?" asked Nicole.

"I don't know, but he looks really familiar. I've seen him before. I just don't know where."

Jade thought long and hard about where she may have seen him before, but she just could not seem to remember. Maybe she had slept with him on one of her drunken nights, but she couldn't quite recall. She thought hard, but her concentration was broken when the starter gun was fired. Jade disregarded the thought and watched the track meet.

The meet was almost over. It was down to the last race, the 400m dash. This was the most anticipated event of the evening because Greg Williams set the new record at Georgia Southern, and Tony Campbell was the reigning champion of the four-hundred-meter race at Elite Relays for the past two years. The guy with the "Tampa Tech Athletics" t-shirt was holding the starting blocks for Tony Campbell, and Jade was so anxious she could barely find the words to tell Nicole.

"Sis, sis… that's him," Jade stuttered. "That's the guy."

"Who? Which one?"

"Him! Right there, holding the starting blocks."

Nicole turned to Jade and said, "Girl, that's Devin Watson."

The gun fired, and the runners exploded out of their starting blocks. Everyone at the meet watched the race from start to finish, knowing they were about to witness history. Everyone except Jade. She didn't care about anything around her. All she was concerned about was finally putting a face to a name. Devin Watson.

The race was over, and Tony Campbell had done it again. The fans were all on their feet, jumping and cheering. Everyone on the field was in awe as they ran up to him for congratulations. Even Nicole was excited, and she had had no idea who Tony was before the race.

Everyone at the meet was excited about the last race. Fans and reporters gathered around Tony. Jade was happy for

Tony as well. But she was more interested in Devin. Jade watched from afar as he gathered her training equipment to leave for the training room.

Inside the training room, the underclassmen's athletic trainers were hard at work, cutting the tape from wrapped ankles, preparing ice bags, and massaging tight muscles. She walked to the counter, placed her bags down, grabbed a pair of scissors, and yelled, "NEXT!" for another athlete to get a wrapping removed. Not only were the trainers assisting athletes from the track meet, but both the men's and women's basketball practice was just ending. The locker room was in full effect. Nicole stood in the corner of the training room, out of the way admiring her sister's passion. In times like these, Nicole wished she had a drive like Jade.

About an hour later, the training room was down to just two athletes. Jade let the rest of the student trainers go for the day. The last two athletes in the training room were female basketball players finishing up their ice therapy. Jade was sweeping the floor and putting all the equipment back in their respective places.

Tony Campbell walked through the double doors.

"I am not too late, am I?" he asked.

"No, it's fine. What do you need?" Jade asked.

"Well, I feel fine, but my boy thinks I need some extra stretching."

"You know he's right," she said. "Stretching after is just as, if not more important than stretching before."

"Wow, you sound just like D-Dub. He's always telling me you're only young for so long, and you only get one pair of legs."

"Sounds like this guy knows a little something about the human anatomy."

Devin walked through the double doors, and Tony yelled, "D-Dub, I told you I was coming to get stretched! You don't have to babysit."

Jade was stunned by the sight of Devin. They made eye contact. Tony began to rant about Devin never taking his word for anything, but both Jade and Devin ignored his child's play. Tony lay on his stomach as Jade massaged his hamstring, but she never took her eyes off Devin. She stood on one side of the table while Devin walked up to the opposite side. Tony was still talking about Devin's lack of trust.

"Hi, how are you, Lil lady?" Devin asked.

Jade was hesitant but managed to say, "I'm just fine. How about you?"

"I'm just making sure hardhead here is doing what I told him to do."

"Despite his current tantrum, he speaks highly of you. D-Dub, right?" said Jade.

"Oh, really?" Devin said, cutting his eye at Greg.

"Well, that's the name everyone calls me back home, but it's Devin Watson. What's your name?"

"Jade Carter. Senior student-athlete trainer."

She was so used to introducing herself with a title, that she said this naturally like it was a part of her actual name. Devin reached out his hand and said good-humoredly, "Nice to meet you, Jade Carter, senior student athletic trainer."

She gave him an uneasy look, ready to retaliate with sarcasm when he cleverly responded, "I'm just teasing, but it's nice to meet you."

Although they both knew this wasn't their first meeting, they still treated it as their initial encounter. Nicole sat in the corner with a smirk on her face. It was hard for her not to bring up the night of the party.

Devin was an average looking guy with a husky build. His skin was light brown, and his dreaded locks were pulled back into a neat ponytail. His big brown eyes looked as if they had many stories to tell. Jade was down to listen to anything he had to tell with his northeastern accent.

"You're all set," Jade told Tony as she tapped the back of his calf.

"I appreciate it, Jade," Tony said as he reached to the ground to put his shoes back on.

"So, since we have something in common, why don't we talk about it over lunch sometime soon?" Devin asked Jade.

Jade blushed. A guy had never asked Jade on a date before. She didn't want to say no but couldn't find the nerve to say yes. Her face looked as if she was going to vomit at any moment. Nicole stepped in and said, "Yeah, when and where?"

Devin took Jade's phone and stored his number. "Whenever you're ready, just let me know."

Jade felt chills run from the crown of her head to the soles of her feet. She felt like she could physically melt into the floor. She wished she really was melting.

"Will do," Jade said

Devin smiled and left the room.

Jade sat down and buried her face in her hands. "I most definitely messed that one up, sis." Nicole was trying not to laugh. "I mean, I can't talk to a guy to save my life, at least not the ones I actually like. I'm glad you were here to save my ass."

Jade wished she could have a real conversation with guys like Nicole could. She made it seem easy like it was natural to her. This was the first time Jade and Nicole were in the same room, and a man showed Jade more attention than Nicole. Jade didn't know how to react to the attention, but she liked it.

Chapter 4

The next day, Nicole and Rachel were in the mall buying new lingerie for their after-dark activities. Rachel was schooling Nicole on what type of attire she should buy to always keep the tricks guessing.

"With your skin tone, you can wear any dark color, but to add to the sex appeal include something bright to compliment your skin tone," Rachel explained to Nicole. "Or to really get them worked up, match all your lingerie but wear an off the wall color pair of heels."

Nicole nodded at everything Rachel was telling her. Once the girls were done in the lingerie store, they went to the shoe department. Nicole was hungry, so she stopped by the hotdog stand while Rachel continued.

Nicole was in line and looking up at the menu board, trying to decide what to order when a man approached her. He went out of his way just to talk to her, even skipping the line. Nicole noticed his awkwardness and giggled under her breath. She was used to seeing guys lose basic cognitive skills when they saw her.

She smirked at him and proceeded ahead in the line to order food. When she tried to pay for her food, he beat her to the punch. He handed the cashier a fifty-dollar bill.

The awkward man finally spoke.

"Hey beautiful, what's your name?"

By this time, she was annoyed, so pretended not to hear him.

"My name is Tyreke, where are you headed?" Now it was obvious that he wasn't going to give up.

"I'm Candy Cane!" Nicole replied.

The man stopped in his tracks and whispered to himself, "Candy Cane?" He ran back to her and asked, "Well, does Candy Cane have a number I can reach her at?"

"No, I'm too busy to talk on the phone or have relationships."

"Busy doing what?"

"Working."

"Where do you work?"

"A club!"

"What club?"

"If you've been there before then you would know." Nicole found the man to be physically attractive, and his persistence made him look even more attractive to her.

"Are you going to tell me the name of it?" Tyreke asked. "There are a lot of clubs around here," he continued sarcastically.

Still trying to blow him off because she really did not have time for a relationship, Nicole said, "If you just so happen to go to the right club on the right night, I just might give you my real name."

Tyreke was stunned by her fierce attitude. He almost gave up. He watched her go into the shoe store and could only shake his head. He had just seen the most beautiful girl in his life and couldn't get her real name.

"Girl, what took you so long?" Rachel asked, having already made her purchases and ready to go.

"You know how these dudes be."

"Well, was he at least cute this time?"

"He was actually very attractive, and he was well put

together," Nicole responded. "But I don't have time for a relationship right now. Plus, who wants to date a stripper?"

The two girls looked at each other and, in sync, said, "Everybody!"

The next morning, Jade was at her apartment, trying to build up the nerve to call Devin. The phone rang three times before he answered, "Devin Watson."

"Hi, I don't know if you remember me or not but this is Jade." She had rehearsed this line time and time again.

"How could I forget Jade Carter, senior student athletic trainer," he said jokingly to break the obvious nervousness in Jade's voice.

She most definitely bought it because she already felt more comfortable. "Ah-ha, so you do remember me? How have you been?"

"I'm good. Just all work and no play," Devin said.

"I know that lifestyle far too well."

"Can you take a break from that busy lifestyle and grab some lunch?"

Jade was completely taken back and didn't know how to answer. "Well, umm, I probably, I don't know. I mean, it's likely." Her nervousness seeped through the phone, and Devin could tell.

"Is that a yes?"

"Yea, yeah, yes. Yes, I will have lunch with you."

"Cool, is one o'clock good for you?"

"Yea, I can eat at one."

Jade hung up the phone and felt her heart drop to her stomach. She had an official date, in the middle of the day, with a guy who was actually interested in her. No guy had ever invited her anywhere but their dorm room or apartment to have sex. This was the first time she ever felt this way. Overly excited, she began to pick out her outfit right away.

She had no idea about how to dress for a first date. She opened her closet and just stared at her bland wardrobe before attempting to choose an article of clothing. Undecided on whether she should wear jeans, shorts, a dress, or a skirt, she pulled a combination of different outfits. After five attempts, she started to look at herself as opposed to the clothes she was wearing.

She stripped down to her panties and bra and stared at herself in a full-length mirror. She critiqued every part of her body, disgusted by every detail. She looked at her face and counted over a dozen blemishes from acne scarring. Her own smile made her cringe. The gap between her two front teeth distracted her from a perfectly aligned, pearly-white smile. Her self-bashing was immediately followed by dreadful childhood memories. Children in grade school would tease her about her enormous gap, so she had asked Michelle for braces.

"I'm not wasting my money on your ugly ass."

She could still hear Michelle's voice in her head over a decade later. Michelle reminded Jade that she was different from Nicole every opportunity she got. Michelle called Jade ugly so much that it was practically embedded in her DNA as an adolescent.

Her eyes moved down her body, now observing her skinny legs and broad shoulders. Before she could look into her own eyes again, there was a tear flowing down her cheek. A picture of her and Nicole on the dresser finally took the mind of her own reflection. She reminisced on her childhood, recalling how everything was always so easy for

Nicole. She always had a boyfriend, and there was always a guy waiting for his chance with her. Jade remembered one specific time when a guy appeared to be overly interested in her. She fell for his sweet talk, but his intention was only to get Nicole's attention. Jade was just an invite for him. She felt used and betrayed; but mostly jealous. She envied all of Nicole's physical attributes, but the one thing she admired the most was Nicole's wit with men.

She always seemed to have them eating out of the palms of her hands, partially because of her beauty and partially because she was charismatic. Jade often had episodes when she compared herself to Nicole, highlighting all her faults and magnifying Nicole's assets. She knew she shouldn't be so hard on herself, but she was so accustomed to it from her childhood that it became a part of who she was.

Time was winding down. Jade needed to leave soon if she wanted to make it to the restaurant by their confirmed time. She settled for a pair of jeans and a cardigan, and then stormed out of the apartment. She sat in the parking lot of the restaurant, double-checking herself in the mirror to waste time, making sure he got there before she did. In her rearview mirror, she saw him get out of his car and watched him walk inside. She looked in the mirror one last time before going inside as well. She entered the building and scanned the room, secretly hoping he was in the restroom so she could tell herself he wasn't there and leave. But she found Devin already seated at a booth. He had not noticed her until she was already sitting down.

"Hey, Miss Lady! How have you been?"

"I'm fine. How about yourself?"

"Enjoying life, one day at a time."

Devin could tell she was nervous. She hid behind the menu, pretending to be uncertain about a food choice. She was extremely shy. Devin took the menu from her and placed it on the table right before looking her in the eyes.

"Relax, I don't bite. I swear," he reassured her.

Jade took a deep breath. She tried to make things as normal as possible, although she was uncomfortable.

"So, you have a Georgia driver's license. What brings you to Florida?"

"I needed to get out of the environment I was in," Devin said. He answered her questions with a strange precaution and extreme vagueness. He had an unhealthy past life but was working to be a better person. He did not want to scare her away because he really did like her.

"Plus, Florida has better opportunities and pretty ladies," he continued.

He made her blush. She admired his charm. She looked into his eyes and instantly wanted to know everything about him. Before she could slow down her brain to form a question, he interrupted her thought process.

"So, why do you train?"

"Ever since I was a little girl, I've had a passion for helping people. Plus, I have a thing for sports. So there you have it, an athletic trainer."

"That's dope."

"I played sports in high school, but I was never any good at any of them. I ran track, played basketball and volleyball. I rode the bench majority of the time, but it didn't bother me." Jade just rambled along and didn't even notice she was doing it. "I was mediocre in my individual events, but my relay team did place at the county meet. I played for about half of every volleyball game, probably because I am so tall."

Jade's rambling was at full speed, and there was no slowing her down. But Devin didn't really mind; he just smiled and listened. "Oh, and basketball was my absolute favorite. Even though I only played for twenty minutes total my whole high school career, it was my favorite of them all. It was probably the interaction, the contact, the adrenaline just something about the orange ball has me hooked. Even now, basketball season is my favorite time of year!"

Jade's nervousness had taken over the conversation, and her excitement got the best of her. By the time she was done talking, the waitress was bringing the food to the table. Jade didn't hesitate. She immediately grabbed a napkin and fork and started to dig in. Devin, on the other hand, bowed his head to bless his meal. The silence made Jade feel awkward; she felt obliged to fill it. Therefore, she lowered her head and closed her eyes.

When Devin was done praying, he looked over at Jade and said, "I hope you're not one of those women who don't like to eat in public." Jade replied with a smirk on her face, "Do I look like I hold back with the fork?"

Jade continued to talk through the meal.

"What do you do?"

"Security mostly," he replied.

"What's your plans after school?"

"I have a couple of local job offers, but I also have a shot at working with Olympians."

"Word?! Now that's mad dope."

He continued to woo her throughout their conversation with little to no effort. Jade was excited about how cool he thought she was. It made her like him even more. An image of them being together occupied her mind. She saw a future with him on their first date.

"I love a headstrong, driven woman."

His hooks were in Jade, and she couldn't shake or deny it. She was falling for Devin on their first date, and she didn't even realize it. Devin knew he had her just where he wanted her. But he remained patient, as he wanted this bond with Jade to be strong before he could tell her exactly who he really was.

Chapter 5

Nicole was staring at her reflection through the light bulb-bordered mirror again. She had already smoked a marijuana joint before coming into Cloey's. This time she wasn't getting high to calm her nerves; she just liked the feeling of it now. She loved the way it made her feel, and being at Cloey's gave her an excuse to smoke it.

Unfortunately, she thought she was only smoking marijuana.

She was almost completely dressed when Rachel came into the dressing room, yelling, "I got that get right!"

Rachel sold pre-rolled joints to the girls at the club as a side hustle. She shared her joints with Nicole, although she never told her or the other girls there was cocaine in them. Rachel had built trust with all the girls, so no one had any reason to question her product.

Nicole and Rachel shared one joint before Nicole went out into the club. This night, she wasn't as picky. She put her ego aside, and money was the only thing on her mind. She had become more efficient and learned to pace herself.

She would do seven dances before going back to the dressing room. She did this for multiple reasons. First, she was full of money, and she didn't want to drop any being greedy. Second, she would feel herself getting tired and sweaty, so she felt the need to freshen up. Lastly, to smoke a half joint or take another shot.

She was in the middle of her dance routine when a well-dressed young man pulled her off the client's lap. The young man threw the guy a twenty-dollar bill so he wouldn't complain about being shorted a dance. Nicole, now drunk and high, didn't initially get a good look at the guy who was pulling her to the bar. Once she sat down, she quickly realized it was Tyreke from the mall.

"Looks like I found you." He yelled over the music.

"Looks like you did, but no one was hiding," she yelled back as she got up and walked away.

He grabbed her waist. She snatched away. "Can't you see I'm working? I don't have time."

He pulled a wad of money from his pocket. "Do you have time now?"

She wanted to say yes, but her ego wouldn't allow her to be bought. The young man was very attractive and didn't dress like the other men in the club. He actually looked displaced. He was dressed in slacks with suspenders, a button-down shirt, and a tie. It was obvious his only business in Cloey's was Nicole.

She finally answered, "Tyreke, right?"

"Yea, that's exactly what I thought," he said.

Nicole was in disbelief. How could someone so eager be so self-centered? She paused before responding. "I will have time tomorrow. I'm all booked up tonight." She left him standing there in his tailored outfit, a fist full of cash, and his pride crushed.

She went back to the locker room for another round of shots. She was interrupted by a tap on the shoulder. It was Cloey, the owner of the club. She pulled Nicole so close that her lips touched Nicole's ear. "Meet me in my office in five minutes."

Cloey intimidated Nicole. She was taller than the average woman and more masculine than the average man. She was forty pounds overweight and was easily mistaken for a bouncer in her own establishment. Nicole had only seen her twice, and both times Cloey was wearing oversized jeans and a basic tee shirt. She wasn't a person of many words, but the few words she did speak were definite. She didn't look like she owned a successful business, but she preferred it that way. Nicole could handle the old perverts in the club. She felt like the power was in her hands to control the situation when dealing with clients. But Cloey made her feel small. Being in Cloey's presence made her feel outside of her body.

Nothing felt real. Her mind was racing. "What could she possibly want? What did I do? What didn't I do? Did I say something wrong or out of line?" All of the questions became overwhelming and unbearable to process.

Nicole finally made it to the locker room. She didn't know if she wanted to take another shot or try to sober up. All she knew was that she needed to go to the office with a clear mind, but she was already loaded. Nicole sat distraught before making a move.

Cloey's office was across the club and up the stairs on the second floor. She stumbled up the four steps into the club. The doorway to the stairwell was so small; it looked like a garbage chute from across the room from where Nicole was standing. With each step, the butterflies in Nicole's stomach fluttered. As she reached the top step, she felt her knees get weak. She knocked on the door.

"Come in!"

She stepped inside the office, and Cloey offered her a seat. Cloey stood up from behind the desk and stood by the window, which overlooked the club.

"Six thousand dollars a week, 24k a month, and still not enough!"

It took a minute for it to register in Nicole's head that Cloey was referring to the money she made as a club owner. She sat there, speechless, unable to understand why Cloey was discussing her finances with the 'new girl.'

Cloey turned around fast and pointed at Nicole.

"But you can change it all."

Now Nicole was extremely puzzled. She wasn't the best at math, but she wondered how her little private, fifteen-dollar dances would make a big difference in Cloey's bank account. "I've been watching you and how these tricks act when you dance with them," Cloey said.

"You've got attitude, girl."

Nicole thought she was about to get cursed out, fired, or both.

"I like it, but pole and private dances aren't really your style," Cloey explained. "And I know it's uncomfortable; that's why you stay high all the time."

Cloey undressed Nicole with her eyes. Nicole squirmed in the chair, and she screamed inside. She was embarrassed because Cloey knew she was taking drugs to work. She wanted to run out of the office so badly.

"I'm not going to beat around the bush with you. It's levels to this life, baby," Cloey explained. "One of my business partners entertains celebrities and rich folks when they come to town. And lately, his entertainment hasn't been...entertaining."

Nicole tried to speak "Do yo-?"

Cloey cut her off and continued. "These rich folks have a mindset that they can have whatever it is they want because they have the big bucks to pay for it. And guess what? We are going to give them whatever they desire." Nicole was still pondering on what her role was in this whole ordeal.

"Basically, Nicole, we will provide a service that will satisfy any sexual encounters they may desire."

Nicole was uneasy about this idea. She was content with dancing, but Cloey was essentially asking her to be a prostitute. She already made her mind up before Cloey even offered the ultimatum.

"They are willing to pay up to fifty thousand dollars. After we split the money, you should make out with at least five thousand each time," Cloey said. "You just need to recruit a few more girls in case a client requests several girls."

Nicole's demeanor completely changed. She was on the edge of her seat, waiting for more information.

"If you can consistently bring at least three girls to every party, those are the numbers you could be making."

Nicole was all in, and it was obvious to Cloey. She walked over to Nicole and officially asked, "Do you want it?"

Nicole was eager to agree. She was about to speak, but Cloey put her fingers on Nicole's lips so she couldn't talk. "Before you decide, sleep on it. I want you to be 100% sure this is what you want."

Nicole left the office, and although she had not spoken one word while she was there, her emotions were everywhere. She decided to leave the club completely for the night. All night long, she thought about the proposal. The idea of asking Jade for advice was out of the question. This was the hardest decision she would have to make in her life so far.

The next morning, Nicole woke up earlier than usual to go to the community college; she recently quit. She needed to clear her mind and make a decision by the end of the day. Not many people knew her because her tenure there had been so short-lived. Luckily her student I.D. was still valid, and she carried a backpack to blend in with the student population.

She sat at a table by herself in a secluded corner in the back of the library. Students and faculty walked in and out of the library as Nicole sat there daydreaming. For the majority of her visit, she didn't think about anything. She was jolted out of the nostalgic state by an unexpected, familiar face.

"I'm starting to think you and I are destined to be together."

Tyreke had noticed Nicole from across the room and couldn't stop himself from approaching her.

"I'm starting to think you are stalking me." She snapped back.

"Do you attend school here?" he asked.

"What kind of person hangs out at a college they don't attend?"

"You'd actually be surprised."

Nicole was instantly annoyed by Tyreke's presence. He spoke proper English and wore shirts with cufflinks. He had a crisp haircut, clean fingernails, and perfectly white teeth. She preferred guys who were rough around the edges, with a trail of marijuana scent nearby. Men of his status and demeanor were not her type.

Tyreke recognized the disconnect between the two and immediately tried to ease the tension in the air.

"How has work been?"

"Well, since you asked, I don't work at the club anymore.

I should be starting my new job very soon."

"Really, what are you going to be doing?"

Nicole knew she couldn't tell him the whole truth, but she had no reason to lie because she barely knew him. She wanted to make this new job appear to be a lot better than dancing half-naked in a room full of desperate men. She said the first thing that came to mind.

"Party promoter." Technically she wasn't lying, but she wasn't telling the whole truth either.

"That sounds exciting! When do you start?"

"Soon. Why are you here?" This was her third time seeing him, and she still didn't know anything about him.

"I'm just helping my dad with this new project he's doing." Tyreke vaguely responded.

"Oh well, have fun. I have to get to my next class, which starts in ten minutes."

"Hold on, wait! At least take my number, and maybe the next time I see you, it will be planned and not by coincidence."

Nicole was skeptical at first but got his number anyways.

Jade woke up with a text message from Devin. "I want to see you today."

She instantly got butterflies, but she didn't want to seem overly eager.

"Name the place and time," Jade replied. "I'll be over in an hour."

Devin didn't specify a place, but Jade didn't care. She liked being around him. Even though they had only hung out once. It was the first time someone really got to know Jade because they genuinely wanted to. The idea of love put Jade in a happy place, even though she didn't exactly know how it felt. The idea of someone showing her individual attention was almost unbearable.

Jade was in a frenzy. She wanted to share the good news with Nicole, but she didn't want to get her hopes up just to be shot down. She was already debating what she would wear. The ice was already broken between her and Devin, but she was still anxious.

It was a sunny day, so shorts, a t-shirt, and sandals were befitting. Her anxiety intensified as she waited for him, checking her phone every other minute. Suddenly, there was a knock at the door. Jade knew it was Devin, but she secretly wanted it to be anyone else.

"Who is it?" she yelled.

She looked through the door hole to find Devin standing on her porch, unwrapping a new stick of gum. She opened the door with a surprised look on her face. They sized one another up, both satisfied with what they saw.

Then Devin took one step closer, wrapped his arms around her waist and hugged her. "Hmm, you smell nice pretty lady."

She let go of him immediately and created a distance between them. "Ready to go?"

Devin was attracted by her bashfulness. "Yes, let's go!"

He opened her door and played soft music while he drove.

Devin was a perfect gentleman, but Jade didn't know how to respond to his kind gestures. They had been riding around the city and had still not spoken a word to each other. They'd only made random eye contact at stop signs and red lights while rhythm and blues from the 90s played through the radio.

Jade had no idea where Devin was taking her, and she didn't care. Just being in Devin's presence put her in an unfamiliar place, which she was becoming acquainted with. It was getting dark, and Devin finally pulled into a drive-thru movie theater.

"What's playing tonight?" Jade asked.

"It is a story about a guy falling in love with a girl at first sight. Kind of like you and I."

Jade wanted to unload all of her emotions on him. His mannerisms and charisma made her even more physically attracted to him. She wanted to know what he was thinking to ensure the feelings were reciprocated before she expressed how she felt about him.

"Why do you like me?" she asked.

"I don't know. It's just something about you."

"Something like what?"

"I really can't call it; it's unexplainable."

Devin was very vague in his response, but Jade didn't care. It was the most she had ever got out of any man, and his reply was enough for her.

It had been three days since Nicole had been back to the club after Cloey's offer. Although she had already made her decision, she was still skeptical. She knew it was morally wrong, but she needed the money. She had asked herself these same questions over and over again, but something still didn't seem quite right. Just when she was about to back out of her decision, she thought of the financial potential.

Nicole was literally driving herself insane. She sat on the edge of the dresser, and just as she did, a quarter fell on the floor, which was when she had a great idea. The only way to settle her conscience was through a simple coin toss. Heads, she would take the job; tails she wouldn't take the job. Either way, she would have to tell Cloey her final decision tonight. She reached down and grabbed the coin. Taking her time, she looked at the coin. She examined it to make sure it was a regular quarter as if she was a referee at the Super Bowl. Taking a deep breath, she finally flipped the coin.

It was the ideal toss, perfect in rotation and with good air time. It almost touched the ceiling. As gravity pulled it down, Rachel yelled, "Nic, where you at?" The coin dropped to the floor, and Nicole took off, full speed to the living room.

"Wassup, girl?" Nicole responded.

"Don't wassup me! Wassup with you? You haven't been to the club, you bugging!"

"Nah, it's nothing. I'm going tonight, though!"

"Oh yeah? Well, Cloey asked about you too," Rachel said with a puzzled look on her face.

Cloey never asked about an individual girl in particular. Rachel had been working at Cloey's since her junior year in high school, and this was a first for her. Nicole knew exactly what Cloey wanted.

"Don't worry. I will be back tonight."

As soon as Nicole entered her bedroom, the first thing that caught her eye was the quarter she had recently flipped. She kneeled down to pick it up. It had landed on heads, It was decided then. She was taking the job and could not go back on it.

Yet again, Nicole was back in the dressing room, preparing herself for "work." Nicole's appearance and demeanor suggested it would be the average day in the club. And in fact, she was fine. She was content with everything.

She had rehearsed her lines for Cloey, and she was ready. The other girls in the room were very uncomfortable, and they made the atmosphere uneasy. Nicole never talked to any of the other girls at the club besides Rachel, so the awkward silence was expected. But this particular night was different from any other time. The tension was so thick, and the envy was so noticeable, Nicole could almost feel the jealousy seeping from their pores.

Her initial thought was, *why now?* What had she done to cause so much friction? Then on second thoughts, she realized she didn't care. She leaned in closer to the mirror and applied more blush. Nicole always acted humble around others, so her peers didn't feel imitated by her physical attributes. Throughout her childhood, she was confident only when necessary.

By her teenage years, she would flirt with conceit. This was the first time, apart from a couple of other occasions, where her confidence would overpower her conscious, and the naturally humble Nicole became arrogant. She never apologized or felt remorse because she was well within her emotional well-being for advocacy. Finalizing her makeup and outfit, she left the dressing room and walked up the stairs entering the club. She really had no idea why the girls were different today. Her concern wouldn't let her conscious relax. It wasn't for the sake of them but for herself. She wondered if they knew about Cloey's offer. Nicole was out of her element mentally. Normally, she worked high, drunk, or both. However, tonight she was sober because she knew she had to confront Cloey, and she wanted to have a clear head.

Upon entering the club, she glanced up to see if Cloey was standing in the big window overlooking the club, but she wasn't. Even the blinds were closed. She proceeded to her first dance of the night, occasionally checking to see if Cloey was in her office. She was uncertain about just going up to the office unexpectedly. Nicole anticipated Cloey looking down, searching the floor of the club, and seeing her so she would feel obligated to go upstairs and talk to her.

Three hours and fifteen dances later, Nicole still had not seen nor talked to Cloey. It was the end of the night, and the club was settling down. Nicole was exhausted. She made her way back to the dressing room, where she found two of the other girls. The tension wasn't as thick as before. It was late, and all the girls were tired, but a stranger could still notice the separation. Nicole changed and was walking back to the car as Cloey pulled up in a Chrysler 300 with 24-inch rims. Nicole never knew what kind of car Cloey drove, but she was certain it was hers because at the top of the windshield, in big, bold lettering read "C L O E Y."

Nicole stopped in mid-stride. She had been sure she wasn't going to see Cloey tonight. She was surprised, nervous, and shocked, but prepared all at the same time. Cloey stepped out of the vehicle in her typical butch attire, Timberland boots, big saggy blue jeans with a polo collar shirt that was obviously four sizes too big. Her dreadlocks were pulled back into a ponytail.

"What's up, baby girl? Long time, no see."

"Well, you know, I've been thinking a lot about what you asked."

Cloey's eyes seemed to have gotten bigger as she stuck her neck out and raised her eyebrow, showing Nicole had all of her attention.

"And?"

"Umm, I, I, umm . . . this stripping shit ain't gonna cut it. I'm tryna make some real money."

A sigh of relief emanated from Cloey like she had been trapped in a cage for years, and someone had finally unlocked the door. Trying to compose herself, she responded, "Good deal."

There was an awkward silence accompanied by a peculiar stare between the two. Their eyes met and locked like two opposing magnetic poles. Cloey looked through Nicole's eyes to her soul and had a conversation with her heart.

Cloey knew Nicole did not want to do the orgy parties. She had only agreed out of fear. She could do without the money because she was making enough stripping. Cloey wanted to explain to Nicole she wasn't made for the job, but she broke eye contact and scanned Nicole's whole body, taking an extra split-second on all her perfect curves. She had carried herself like a man for so long; the logic-over-emotion philosophy had totally taken over her sincerity. All she could see were dollar signs.

"Don't show your face around here anymore," as the words jumped off Cloey's lips,

Nicole felt her body go limp. She thought Cloey didn't need her any longer.

"I will call you in a week. Meanwhile, build a team," And just like Cloey had knocked her ego down, she lifted her spirits just as fast. "We're going to the top."

Rachel was now outside. She had missed the majority of the conversation; the only part she had caught was, "We're going to the top."

Nonchalantly she said, "Yall can go to the top some other time, but tonight we are going home." She was referring to herself and Nicole.

Her voice startled Nicole. She was going to verbally agree with Cloey, but she didn't want Rachel to find out. Nicole nodded her head at Cloey. Cloey returned the gesture with a wink. Their non-verbal cues confirmed a mutual agreement and understanding between the two.

Nicole smiled the entire trip to their apartment. There was an awkward silence between Nicole and Rachel. Rachel knew there was something suspicious going on between Nicole and Cloey.

She wanted to ask Nicole what she and Cloey had been talking about, but she knew she wouldn't get an honest answer. Nicole was obviously somewhere else mentally during the ride home. To break the silence, Rachel asked, "how much did you make tonight?"

"Huh?" Nicole paused for a split second. "Oh, you know. The usual," she answered.

"It might be time for you to get some wheels," Rachel responded. "Hell, you can afford it, especially since we're splitting the rent."

"Nah, I'm thinking I might be able to get my own place real soon."

Nicole was telling Rachel things she had not intended to.

"How are you gonna do that, Ms. Lady?"

"I got this new job I'm about to start, and it pays very well," Nicole answered.

Although Nicole didn't say exactly what kind of job and Rachel didn't know the exact job either, she knew Cloey was involved somehow. Rachel put a mental barrier in the car between her and Nicole. She felt betrayed by both Cloey and Nicole. There was nothing she could do about it. Meanwhile, Nicole was on cloud nine and didn't even realize the state her friendship with Rachel was in.

Chapter 6

There was a knock at Jade's door, and she had no idea who it could be. She practically wished it was Devin. She knew it couldn't be him because he was out of town for a seminar. Before she could imagine anyone else, she had already opened it.

To her surprise, it was Michelle. The only other time Michelle had visited Jade's apartment had been at her house-warming party, two years ago. Jade knew why Michelle visited the first time, but this time she was puzzled beyond belief.

"What are you doing here, Mom?"

"Can't I come by and see how my big girl is doing?" Michelle responded.

"Yeah, you can, but you never have before," Jade said.

"Well, here I am! How are you?"

Jade was confused by this peculiar situation. Michelle never showed interest in her well-being, and she didn't know how to respond. She felt like she was being set up, and no matter how she answered the question, her response wouldn't be what Michelle wanted to hear. Therefore, she responded as conservatively as possible.

"The normal. Work and school."

"Work, huh? How's that? You're a trainer, right?" Michelle answered her own question.

By this time, Jade figured Michelle was interested in more than just work and school.

"How have you been?" Jade asked Michelle.

"I do what I can when I can do it," Michelle responded. Now Jade was fully aware something was not right.

"What does that mean, Mom?" Michelle could hear the aggravation in Jade's voice.

Michelle took a seat on Jade's living room sofa and pulled back her sweater sleeves high enough that Jade could notice the needle injections on her left arm. Michelle saw Jade's eyes connect with her arm, and she immediately pulled the sleeves back down.

"I lost my job! I am four months behind in mortgage, and Chris is going to leave me." Michelle said in one breath, with no hesitation. "I am desperate; can you help me? I need $2500."

"Bye, mom," Jade said.

Michelle stood up from the sofa and said, "I can pay you back! It will just take some time."

"Bye, mom!"

Jade said again.

Michelle heard the seriousness in Jade's voice and sadly responded, "OK." Jade closed the door behind her, turned her back to the door, and allowed her feet to slide from beneath her until her buttocks touched the floor. She couldn't believe what had just happened. Of all people, her mother was asking for her help out of desperation, and she did not feel the desire to help. In her heart, she felt a genetic obligation, but her brain reminded her of their relationship.

She allowed herself to slip into a daze and reminisce about a specific day during her childhood. Jade had come to live with Michelle and Nicole when she was ten years old after the death of her grandmother, Michelle's mother. Michelle took her two daughters shopping for clothes as the school year was nearing. Nicole was allowed to pick out clothes at high-end department stores while Jade was told there was only enough money for her to shop at thrift stores and wear Michelle's hand-me-downs, which were two sizes too big. This memory accompanied many other similar ones from Jade's childhood, and she still rankled at the obvious mistreatment she had endured.

Jade was good at bottling up her feelings when it came to Michelle, but this situation was new to her. She was used to the emotional abuse, the taunting, the belittling. But instead, she was asking for help, and Jade didn't know how to respond. Although she knew she would get a biased opinion, she called Nicole anyways. She called three times back to back, leaving a voicemail each time along with a text message.

"Nic, call me ASAP!"

Her natural reaction was to call Devin next, but her common sense stopped her, and she instead sent him a text message as well, "Hi babe, I hope you're enjoying yourself! I miss you!"

She needed to talk to someone, but the only two people she felt comfortable opening up to were unavailable. She resorted to what always set her free, always listened to her and never left her alone. Vodka. Jade was not an alcoholic. She only relied on it occasionally, specifically in times of distress. She didn't drink very often - in fact; she hadn't drunk since she started seeing Devin. When she did drink, she would binge so tremendously that the morning after she would swear off drinking, until, of course, she did it again. After three and a half hours of shots and mixed drinks, in addition to reminiscing on her horrible childhood and sulking in her own misery, Jade finally passed out across her living room table.

Nicole arrived at Jade's door, and just before attempting to ring the doorbell, she remembered Jade had given her a key. Nicole unlocked the door and entered the apartment only to find her big sister still passed out in the living room. Nicole didn't panic because this wasn't the first time she had found Jade in this state. She took a deep breath, put her bags down, and lifted her sister onto the sofa. She went to the kitchen, started a pot of coffee, and wet a washcloth for Jade's forehead. She sat next to Jade on the sofa, gently dabbing her face with the washcloth.

Jade managed to utter, "What time is it? 1:48 pm!" She

moaned. "Ugh, I missed class."

"Don't worry about that; you can make it up. What happened?" Nicole tried to console her.

Jade sat up straight on the sofa, took the washcloth from Nicole, and threw it on the table. Jade was so independent that she didn't know how to recognize when someone was comforting her, not even her own sister. Nicole was aware of this but always tried anyways. Although neither of the girls said anything, their eye contact and facial expressions said everything needed to be told.

"So what's going on, sis?" Nicole asked empathetically.

"Well, your mother came by yesterday." Jade never acknowledged Michelle as her own mother when she wasn't around, mostly because she didn't feel like they shared a mother-daughter relationship. The only reason she did it while she was around Michelle was to limit confrontation.

"That's a surprise. What did she say?" Nicole asked. "You know what, she probably just wanted to see how you were doing," she continued before Jade had a chance to respond. "She's just lonely since I left home, and she lives in that big house by herself now."

All Jade could do was lower her head and nod in disappointment. She could feel her brain shifting, causing her head to pound even harder, making her dizzier and more nauseous. Nicole was about to say something else when Jade shouted, "No, Nicole! She is in trouble. She asked me for money."

Nicole paused for a moment before responding. She didn't want to believe what Jade was telling her. She was in denial, and like every other time, Jade tried to tell her something about their mother.

"You know y'all never got along. Maybe she was just trying to make conversation?" Nicole tried to make an excuse, but by the looks on Jade's face, she knew it wasn't working.

"You should go see her. Don't tell her I sent you; it's just a courtesy visit."

"Why would she ask you for money when she works at the clinic and makes five times more than you?" Nicole asked.

Nicole was angry and confused, trying to fathom the thought of her mother asking Jade for anything. Nicole saw Michelle as a role model who had made ends meet by any means necessary as a single mother. She had witnessed her mother maneuver through the welfare system and finesse her way through any obstacle. Some part of her knew it was morally wrong, but she saw it as a means of survival.

At this point, Jade knew there was nothing she could say to make Nicole believe her.

"Nic, calm down and go see your mother. She would want to see you right now."

This only made Nicole angrier.

"What do you mean, 'see *me*?' You're her daughter too. It's not my fault; she loves me and not you."

Throughout their childhood, it had been obvious that Michelle treated Jade and Nicole differently, but it was an unwritten rule no one questioned why Michelle would verbally and emotionally abuse Jade. This was the first time Nicole ever mentioned the obvious.

Jade was hurt but not surprised. She expected Nicole to break a long time ago, and when she never did, Jade pushed the thought in the back of her mind. She was mentally prepared but not emotionally. The words fell off Nicole's lips as if they were on a suicide mission falling off a cliff, only to be greeted with sharp rocks shattering and penetrating Jade's feelings. Just as violent and painful as actual death, Nicole's words cut Jade's soul leaving it dismayed and inevitably dead. They looked into each other's eyes, Nicole's fiery and fierce, Jade's cold and hard. Nicole's eyes were illuminated with an evil gaze; she was out for blood. She was heartless and fueled by rage.

She was willing to defend and protect her mother, although she knew in the back of her mind Jade was right. Although she was 18 and a legal adult, she had the mindset of a naïve 12-year-old who thought whatever her mother did was right. She was guided by ignorance because she was afraid of the truth.

When Jade was 14, she decided fear was a choice, and as a teenager, she accepted the truth about Michelle. She hated her. Jade was cold. She lacked emotion as she stared into Nicole's burning eyes. Her fire began to melt Jade's iceberg, but Jade was still furious. Jade's breathing became more rapid, and her adrenaline started to flow. What momentarily was only a sculpted piece of clay was regaining life. The difference between Nicole and Jade was merely their levels of self-control. Jade's soul was reanimated. She swallowed hard, and instead of pouncing on Nicole and beating her within an inch of existence, she uttered, from the depths of her soul, "GET OUT!"

They never broke eye contact until Nicole's point of departure. Nicole exited the apartment and slammed the door behind her.

Jade was left on the couch, still in disbelief. Once she was all alone, she wanted to burst into tears, but her pride wouldn't allow her to. Every time she felt an ounce of sadness, she remembered her childhood and decided that was enough misery for a lifetime. She found a way to cheer up. Devin's flight landed in four hours, and she wanted his welcome to be great, so she focused on him and not the situation at hand.

Nicole and Jade handled situations differently. While Jade was at her apartment, level-headed, Nicole was doing a lot worse. Although she had the power as the initiator of the confrontation, she couldn't handle it. When she left Jade's apartment, she couldn't keep her composure. Before she had even made it to the bus stop, she was wearing a face full of tears. Her mind was traveling at 100 mph, and her emotions were haywire. She tried to collect herself before the bus arrived. Being fair-skinned, her face turned red, and her eyes got puffy as she cried. She just wanted to be left alone, but unfortunately, she had to be on public transportation, where it seemed like she was always the center of attention.

Nicole sat down at the bus stop bench and buried her face in her hands. She tried to stop the tears from falling, but she couldn't control them. Occasionally, she would look down the street to see if the bus was coming. She checked once more and noticed it was about three blocks away. Desperately, she tried to compose herself before the bus arrived. She wished she was not there; she wished she was anywhere except the situation she was currently in.

She took two deep breaths, and before she could look up, she heard a voice yell, "Hey, come on!"

She finally looked up, and it was Tyreke in a convertible. She didn't hesitate to occupy his passenger seat. The wind blew through Nicole's hair, drying her teary eyes and landing a smile on her face. Tyreke reached over and grabbed a pair of sunglasses from the glove compartment, and Nicole smiled again as he handed them to her. She felt invisible behind the sunglasses, and she was content with that. Tyreke noticed her joyous mood from his peripherals, and it made him feel a sensation of empowerment like he was invincible. Although her happiness was false, she masked her pain well. Simply being with Nicole made Tyreke happy.

Nicole had been riding with Tyreke for a while before she realized she had no idea where they were going. They were caught at a traffic light, and Nicole finally asked, "Where are we going?"

Tyreke replied, "Where would you like to go?"

Nicole, awed by his response, paused before she said, "Um, surprise me."

Tyreke was even more surprised at her answer. He was speechless as his mind raced. All he could do was nod and smile.

Nicole was a big mystery to him. Unlike any other woman he dealt with, she actually put up a challenge. They got caught by another traffic light, and Nicole asked again, "So where are we going?"

Tyreke wanted to get even with a sarcastic response, but instead, he flashed her a charming smile, loosened his tie, and unfastened his top button. His gesture ate at Nicole. She no longer had control, and Tyreke was well aware of the power shift. Tyreke was also aware she wasn't the average girl he usually dated. He couldn't attract her with his "suit and tie" attire, nor with his bank account. He knew he had to show her the real him in order for her to show him the real her.

Although she had a face that should be on the cover of a magazine, she was just an ordinary girl, so he had to come down to her level. He still couldn't decide where to go. He was out of his element. He was used to wining and dining women, but Nicole was different.

It came to him all at once. On Tuesday and Thursday evenings, underprivileged teenagers performed at the Town Centre, showing off their musical talents. Tyreke only knew this because it was one of his charities he donated to.

When Tyreke turned to enter the shopping district, Nicole was certain he was taking her shopping. She cut her eyes at him from the passenger seat and smirking, murmured under her breath, "Typical." She looked out the passenger window, trying to act nonchalant. By the time they were in the parking garage, dusk had already set in. After parking, they took the elevator to the second floor to the outdoor corridor. Nicole was headed towards the department stores when Tyreke grabbed her hand and redirected her towards the food court.

Puzzled, she giggled and asked, "Are we getting food?"

Tyreke responded. "You told me to surprise you!"

She didn't say anything else but was eager to know what was next. By the time Nicole could smell the food, she was totally convinced they were going to eat. Tyreke grabbed her hand, intertwining his fingers with hers, guiding her down the escalator. The escalator was right in the middle of the courtyard, and Tyreke's timing couldn't have been more perfect. They were coming down the escalator, and the performance was just beginning.

The kids came from every direction, all creating a different beat to contribute to the overall unique sound, but still managed to remain united as one. Some were using trash cans, others buckets and drumsticks, or even something as simple as clapping their hands, stomping their feet, or creating a distinct sound with their mouths.

Every individual beat was in sync and precise to create the perfect sound. Before Nicole and Tyreke reached the bottom of the escalator, a crowd had already gathered. The performers weren't all together congregated on a stage; instead, they allowed their raw talent to flow through the audience. Each performer mingled in the crowd with an individual person in the audience. A group of performers using trash cans made a circle around Nicole and Tyreke.

The percussion got softer, and a young girl - about twelve-years-old - started to play the keyboard. The percussionists danced around the couple, making them the center of attention. It was magical. Everything was flawless like it was taken from the scene of a Hollywood movie or a choreographed play. The moment was unforgettable, and to top it all off, one of the performers recognized Tyreke and shook his hand.

Personally, it wasn't a big deal to Tyreke because he was used to that sort of thing. Nicole, on the other hand, had finally found attraction in his status. Just like in her high school days, ordinary guys never got her attention. After a while, guys with a higher status in life were the only guys who approached her. So, at this moment, being the center of attention was what she desired, and yet again, she felt completely conquered. If there was any doubt in Nicole's mind about Tyreke, it had been voided. He was not special to her; he was just like the average guy she had previously been involved with. Nothing was ever mutual in Nicole's "relationships." She was always looking to benefit from them in some way or the other. Tyreke would be no different. But in Tyreke's head, he was winning. Distracted by her facial features, he wasn't aware that he would become a pawn in Nicole's big game of life.

By the time the performance and the impromptu "meet and greet" between Tyreke and all the kids had ended, Nicole was starving. Her stomach informed Tyreke of the fact as it growled loud enough for him to hear.

"Sounds like someone missed a meal," Tyreke said sarcastically. Nicole couldn't respond. She only blushed.

"Well, I know a little pizza spot, and I promise they don't miss."

Tyreke didn't know he didn't have to impress her anymore. She had already decided to sleep with him. Although she had prematurely made her decision, she still enjoyed his proper etiquette and elegant behavior. So she wasn't going to stop him from being nice. They pulled into the parking lot, and chivalrously, he opened the car door and the door to the restaurant. They sat and ate pizza. The chemistry between the two was starting to flow. Tyreke was on his A-game, while Nicole was just being herself.

Nicole's authenticity had been perfected ages ago; it was so flawless and natural. She could charm anyone, and she did it effortlessly. She lured Tyreke in so deep he could not control himself any longer. Although his chivalry act wasn't fake, he stepped outside of his gentlemanly element and unmasked his real feelings.

"Nicole, we have spent all day together. I am having the time of my life. I have never caught feelings for a girl as fast as I have for you. When I first saw you, I thought I could make you mine, but today I am certain I want you."

She'd heard this kind of confession before. After the attention-filled day, if it wasn't obvious she wanted to have sex, the guy would reveal his true intentions. Although she had previously seen this routine, she had Tyreke all wrong. He had real feelings for her. He was not looking for a one-night stand; he was looking for commitment. He wanted love.

"Well, I have a confession," Nicole blushed. "I've come to the conclusion I want you too." She looked into his eyes and tried not to smile, but she couldn't help herself.

There was an awkward silence, followed by a long and an even more awkward stare before Tyreke extended his upper body across the table and kissed Nicole. Although the kiss surprised Nicole, it was exactly what she needed. She had forgotten about the fight with Jade from earlier. Nothing else mattered to her at this special moment in time.

She was starting to feel a connection in the kiss and jerked backward. Her motive was to reel guys in and have them wrapped up into her to the point of no return until she decided they weren't worth her time anymore. Normally, the goal was made a reality after sleeping with a guy, but with Tyreke, it was different. He was hooked after the first kiss. Both of them were getting involved with something neither of them was ready for.

After the jerk, she sat with her back to the chair, and cunningly asked, "Ready to go?"

Without a verbal response, he stood up, grabbed her hand, and escorted her to his car. Ten minutes into the ride home, Tyreke asked, "Where do you live?" Nicole didn't understand. When she told him she wanted him, she thought he was picking up what she was putting down, but they were obviously on different pages.

Therefore, she put down something else to see if he would pick it up. "My roommate has family in town, so I told her I would stay with a friend."

He responded with, "Am I the friend you are staying with?"

Tyreke did not read between the lines, but Nicole definitely thought he did. She just smiled with a devilish look and hunched her shoulders. The remainder of the ride to Tyreke's house was silent yet heated. Nicole's desire for him was boiling.

Her body temperature rose, and she felt her heart rate increase. She wanted to rip his shirt off as she felt the moisture from her vagina wet her pants. Meanwhile, Tyreke had no idea she was fiercely fighting temptation. He was under the impression his "friend, soon to be girlfriend" was just spending the night. His idea of a good time consisted of the couple watching a movie together and Nicole eventually falling asleep in his arms. The imagery of the sight appeared in his head, and it warmed his heart. Nicole just so happened to look over at him and saw a grin on his face, puzzled she had to ask.

"What are you thinking about?"

Tyreke didn't want Nicole to know just how much he had grown attached to her. Therefore telling her the truth was not an option. But, at the same time, he didn't want to lie to her either. Quick on his feet, he just watered down the truth.

"The morning after," he responded.

Nicole reached towards him, and only the restraint of the seatbelt held her back. She wanted him now more than ever. She tried to keep her composure by crossing her legs and tapping her feet on the car floors. At this point, Tyreke had no idea as to what was going on, and he said, "We are right around the corner from my house."

He pulled into the driveway of his two-story home. Before he could park the car, Nicole was already out of her seatbelt and opening the car door. Tyreke did not know why she suddenly had this sense of urgency. He grabbed a suitcase from the trunk of the car before proceeding to the front door of the house. He reached the doorstep and shuffled through his ring of keys. Finally, he found the house key and scrambled to put it in the lock. The door was unlocked, and he twisted the knob and pushed the door simultaneously. Although the total process only took about 30 seconds, to Nicole, it seemed like an eternity. Halfway through the door, she grabbed him around the waist and kissed the back of his neck. He only laughed and continued walking to the light switch.

He turned around to find Nicole unfastening her own belt. Taken by total surprise, a million thoughts raced through his mind. She completely unfastened her pants and seductively rubbed her hands down the skin of her perfectly toned legs, caressing her curves while stepping out of her shoes. As she stood at his door with only lace boy shorts, Tyreke already had an erection. Out of all the millions of thoughts running through his mind, he managed to stutter,

"Wha-wha-what you doing?"

Stunted by Nicole's bold actions, the young man couldn't even speak proper English. By this time, his innocence was not only cute and adorable, but it also turned Nicole on even more. She walked in his direction, and his erection grew to the point that Nicole noticed. Once she was within arm's reach, he grabbed her waist and pulled her to him.

She could feel the bulge in his pants on her lower back, which only made her feminine juices flow heavier. He held her waist as he slid his tongue from her earlobes, down her neck, to the back of her shoulders. Once he reached the edge of her shoulder, he kissed her in the opposite direction. He repeated this motion twice. Each time he reached her ear lobe, it sent a tingling sensation down her spine.

By the third time, she was unfastening his belt from behind her. Once his pants were completely unfastened, he bit the left side of her neck and dropped his pants to his ankles. When she heard the belt buckle hit the tile floor, she reached behind her once more to feel his penis. Stroking him and satisfied with his anatomy's size, she looked over her shoulder and whispered, "I wanna feel it!"

She spread her legs and bent over, arching her back all at the same time. Tyreke stared down at her perfectly shaped behind. He had known this particular event would happen; he just didn't know it would happen so soon. He grabbed her waist, pulling her into him. He was too excited by this point, and he knew he was in for an immediate surprise, but he did not want their first encounter to be a disappointment. So he just caressed her waistline for a while to calm himself down a little. Then he made his way inside of her with each hand on her cheeks. He rubbed her clitoris, making her just as excited as him.

Immediately following the ultimate pleasure, Tyreke took his shoes off and stepped out of his pants, which had been around his ankles the entire time. Then he carried Nicole to his bedroom, where the two slept naked. It wasn't long after they had lain down that Tyreke was sound asleep. Nicole laid there in his arms for an hour or so before easing herself away from him and inching out of bed. It was as if she had an extra sense because as soon as she checked her phone for the time, Cloey called.

"Where you at?" she asked.

"Westwood," she responded.

Someone had to be in a certain tax bracket to live in Westwood. Cloey was confused but was also being nosey. She asked, "What are you doing out there?"

Nicole didn't want to lie, but she certainly didn't want to tell the truth.

"Nevermind, just text me the address, and I will have someone pick you up."

Cloey's attitude instilled fear in Nicole, but she didn't want to spend the night with Tyreke, so she agreed.

Chapter 7

Devin awakened Jade with a text message. "Morning, pretty lady."

When she picked him up from the airport the night before, he seemed so overwhelmed about his trip. Jade didn't want to bring down his high spirits. Therefore, she decided to postpone the venting session she had for him.

Actually, she would probably just push it in the back of her mind, like she did everything else. Avoidance was her refuge. She had depended on it for most, if not all, of her life. She always knew it would all catch up with her one day, but quite frankly, her past was the least of her worries. Her avoidance was a temporary solution, and Jade was well aware of it.

"I'm fine, how are you?" she finally replied.

"Dinner tonight? Be ready by 8 p.m."

Jade blushed as she read the text messages from Devin. No one had ever made dinner plans for her. Every time she went on a dinner date, it was for all the wrong reasons. It was always her idea, or she wasn't directly asked. The one time she was asked, it had been a midnight invitation to Waffle House. She was strictly a booty call. Jade's mind was all over the place. How should she act? What should she wear? How should she style her hair? Before she could ask herself the question aloud, she had already answered herself by planning out a pampering day to prepare herself for the big night.

She had a free spa day gift card she'd kept for three years. Today was the first real reason she could use it. And so, she enjoyed all of the extravagant incentives. After getting catered to and made over for a few hours, she felt so great that she decided to buy a new dress just for the date.

Jade was feeling herself so much; she withdrew money from her emergency fund account to ensure she didn't settle when deciding on a dress.

She walked into multiple stores, her confidence high, searching for the perfect dress. Her eye was captured by the first store she walked into; she was beckoned by a beautiful shiny, gold gown with a deep cut in the front to expose her cleavage, the back and shoulders out. She found a salesperson and politely asked for a size twelve.

A petite Caucasian woman sized Jade up. It immediately made her uncomfortable. "I don't think the dress comes in that size, but I will check anyway."

Jade began to look at other dresses as she waited for the saleswoman to return. She was losing confidence in herself. Finally, she returned with the dress in the right size. The woman handed her the dress with an empty look on her face.

"Where are your dressing rooms, ma'am?" Jade asked politely.

The woman pointed to the back corner of the store, treating Jade with obvious distance. She went into the dressing room to try out the dress.

She shimmied and squirmed into the dress. It fit her but with minimal room. She stared at her own reflection in the mirror for a long while, trying to decide how she felt about the dress. She did not feel like herself and was on the fence about purchasing it. So she wanted someone else's opinion.

She walked out of the dressing room and asked the first person she saw how she looked in the dress. It was a middle-aged woman with skin kissed by the sun, and she replied, "It's not about what I think, honey. It is about how you feel in the dress. Do you feel beautiful while you are wearing it?"

What seemed like a simple question resonated with Jade more than she could mentally process. "Do I feel beautiful? How does 'beautiful' even feel? Have I ever felt beautiful?"

Jade went back into the dressing room and looked into the mirror once more. The longer she looked at herself, the more she looked at her skin, her broad shoulders, and her plush lips and wide nose. She was insecure in her own skin.

She took the dress off and ended up choosing a blander dress that covered her cleavage and stopped below her knees. There was nothing special about it, just like Jade thought there was nothing special about her.

It was already 5:30, and Jade was finally satisfied with the most simplistic dress and matching shoes she could find. She was now heading home and had all the pieces to make herself into a masterpiece.

She took her time to prepare herself. She was in no rush. She took a bubble bath and put on her favorite playlist. She wanted to make sure everything was perfect, from her hair, her make-up, her dress to her shoes. Jade looked at her reflection in a full-length mirror and was impressed with who was looking back at her. She thought about what the woman asked her in the store earlier that day. Although she settled for a more reserved look, she thought to herself, "If beautiful was a feeling, this must be how it feels."

Most of the time, she was only partially satisfied with herself. She sprayed herself with perfume, and it was almost as if Devin knew exactly when she was completely ready because the doorbell rang just in time. Again, just as she had been all day, she was in no rush as she walked through the living room to answer the door. She took her time; after all, she already knew it was Devin, and she did not want to increase her heart rate anymore. Her heart was already racing at an unbelievably high rate.

At the last second, she began to doubt herself. What if I'm over-dressed? What if I'm underdressed? Are my heels too high? What if he doesn't like my hair? Did I put on too much makeup? The questions ran through Jade's mind so fast she couldn't even keep up with them. But it was far too late to back out now. She was completely dressed and had spent an entire day pampering herself. She couldn't allow her low self-esteem and insecurities to tell her otherwise. She took a deep breath and opened the door.

Devin was standing there in khaki pants and a dark blue cardigan with white trim and boots. Jade had never seen Devin outside of sweatpants, and she was impressed with his casual side. But nothing was more impressive than Jade. She was wearing a burnt orange dress that complemented her body impeccably. She was a muscular woman. Her dress was sleeveless, exposing her well-defined arms and broad shoulders.

She wasn't a very curvy woman, but the dress hugged her body, displaying the shape of her body. Jade was pretty much straight up and down, but her huge thighs and broad shoulders made her waist appear smaller than it really was. Jade was glowing, and Devin had a sparkle in his eyes. Both of them were very much satisfied with each other. Being the gentleman he had been since day one, he grabbed her hand and said, "Your chariot awaits." He guided her to the parking lot with his other hand.

Jade knew it wasn't an actual chariot and was more than likely just his everyday vehicle. But it didn't matter to her. She would have ridden on the back of an electric scooter and followed him to the moon. It may have been his everyday vehicle, but that wasn't an excuse for him to compromise his manners or become anything less than a perfect gentleman. He held Jade's hand all the way to the passenger side of the vehicle and didn't let go until after he had opened the door. When she was seated, he reached his head in and gave her a soft kiss on the lips. Jade felt tingles from her lips to her toes. There was even a little delay between her thighs, making her vagina moist and her vulnerable. He stood straight up and walked around to the driver's side of the car. Jade touched her lips partially in disbelief, convinced she was living out a fairy tale.

On the way to the restaurant, neither of them verbally said a word to one another. Soft music played through the radio. Although they said nothing, their body language spoke volumes. Their outer appearance didn't seem out of the ordinary, but inside, their hearts were pounding, and body temperatures rising. Both of them felt overwhelmed with the same spark of curiosity.

This particular type of outing was a first for Jade. No other guy had ever paid her so much attention, and because it was new to her, she didn't know how to accept it. On the other hand, Devin's curiosity was fueled by her opposition to the situation. Jade shared his career interests, which was the norm for him because he had dated within his field before. What really sparked his interest was her diversity. This was their third encounter in a different atmosphere, and he had been impressed every time. Devin was interested in how far their formal outing would go. This was not his first one, but he was not an expert at it either.

He was clueless about the fact that this was her first time. Their innocence and lack of knowledge were what made their interactions stick. The possibilities were boundless. Devin pulled up to an upscale restaurant Jade had only dreamt of. They were greeted by a valet at the entrance. The valet opened Devin's door, and he walked around to Jade's door. He was consistent. Jade felt special as she walked up to the entrance of the restaurant.

She embraced the moment and put a little extra bounce in her step, switching her hips back and forth with every step. Devin was just as caught in the moment as she was, if not more. He had an extra spring in his step too, and he cradled her hand in his as if they were newlyweds walking down the aisle. He felt like a winner to have a lady such as Jade on his arm. In his mind, he had already recognized her as his girlfriend, and they were now an item.

He was proud to have her by his side and wanted to alert the world of his feelings and emotions. He envisioned him interlocking his fingers with hers, raising both arms in the air and screaming, "THIS IS MY WOMAN!"

His brain snapped back to reality, and he just played it cool as they approached the podium, and he said, "Devin Watson, reservation for two."

The greeter looked at the highly confident couple and directed them to a table prepared for two, with white table cloths and lit candles. Devin pulled Jade's chair so she could sit before taking his own seat. They sat at the table across from each and gazed at one another. As they looked into each other's eyes, neither of them could believe their luck. The atmosphere was hypnotizing, and even though the room was filled with people at their dinner tables, to Devin and Jade, it felt as though they were the only two there.

The room was dimly lit, and the candlelight set the mood. The way the candlelight reflected off Jade's face complemented her sun-kissed complexion and magnified the sparkle in her eyes. Devin's skin wasn't as blessed by the sun as Jade's, but the candlelight reflected off his skin too. They were a match made in heaven, and they complemented each other well. The waiter approached the dinner table and began introducing a couple of their signature dishes, but Jade and Devin never broke eye contact. It was as if the waiter wasn't even there. After he finished his rehearsed advertisement, he placed menus on the table and walked away. The couple stared into each other's eyes for a minute longer before Devin broke their hypnosis with, "What are you having?"

Jade picked up the menu, and it looked like a foreign language to her. She scanned the entire thing, just trying to identify something familiar. She finally ran across something she had heard once before in a movie. Sounding it out, she finally replied, "Filet mignon, I mean, I've always wanted to try the filet mignon."

The uncertainty in Jade's voice put a puzzled look on Devin's face.

"Well, I'm glad to be present during your first experience, so I will have one as well." Jade just smiled. She had no idea what she was getting herself into.

"I am a huge fan of fish when it comes to eating clean," Jade muttered

Devin giggled at her innocent ignorance. It was cute, yet attractive to him that Jade thought filet mignon was a fish.

Getting away from the subject, Devin asked, "Are you excited about graduating?"

He expected just a yes or no, but he was surprised by how excited she got with her response.

"Weeeelllllll," Jade responded, stretching out the word. "It's kind of bittersweet. Tech has been my home for the past four and a half, nearly five years now. The people I have met and who have mentored me along the way... they welcomed me without hesitation and treated me like family."

She paused for a second and then continued, "They've treated me better than family. The atmosphere of the school is great, and game side access at every sporting event made me feel a part of the team. The coaches are great; the athletes are even better. I'm going to miss Tech. Although they've offered me a permanent position, I have to leave in order for me to reach the pinnacles I have to reach."

Devin interrupted her, "If it's so bad for you here, why did you decide to stay near home for college?"

At this point, Jade was an open book. There were no filters nor restrictions on what she might say. But she trusted Devin, which was a problem for her. She trusted people without really knowing who they were. They didn't have to earn it. She was innocent and naive. Trust was her gift to the human race, for the simple fact that they were human. She believed they deserved it.

"I'm at home here, but the same reason I stay is the same reason I want and need to leave. I've been hurt more than you can ever imagine."

Before Jade knew it, she had begun to vent. It was like she was outside her own body watching herself from afar. She wanted to stop but she couldn't. She wanted her consciousness to put its hand over her mouth or maybe zip her lips together. It was like second nature to her, and she could not help it. She could not stop it, literally.

"I was raised by my grandmother until she died when I was ten years old. Then I was forced to live with my biological mother. By the way, my mother hates me, but that's a different story. She says I am the reason for all of her downfalls in life because I was conceived during a one-night stand. We don't really have a relationship; we were just forced to be together due to genetic make-up."

A little puzzled now, Devin interrupted and asked, "This does not explain why you still stayed here."

"You did not allow me to finish," said Jade. "I have a little sister, Nicole. She is the spitting image of my mother, but I will go to hell and back for her. Besides my grandmother, I feel like she is the only person in the world I ever loved. But the love for the two is different."

Noticing an even more puzzled look on Devin's face, Jade had no problem explaining how she thought love was.

"It's like I love my grandmother because she nurtured me. She talked to me, she saw me. I was somebody to her. But then there is Nicole. Like I love everything about her. She is so beautiful. She has a perfect smile, a big butt, and small feet. Everything was always easy for her, and everyone loves her too. Sometimes I wish I was her."

Devin just assumed she was exaggerating - a typical case of sibling rivalry.

"I have an older brother, and he is pretty much my role model. He is very successful, and sometimes I wish I was him. But then I accept me for me and try to be the best Devin

I can be. It took me a while to get to the point I am at now. So I'm sure you will eventually get there too. It just takes time."

He grabbed her hand from across the table.

"I can help you get there if you want me to."

There was a major miscommunication, here but Jade agreed with him out loud. Devin was showing her more affection and concern than two people combined in her entire life. Their sparkling eyes connected again, and they were caught in a daze.

Now knowing her story, he wanted to show her better than what she had experienced in her past, and she was ready to allow him to do so. Although they hadn't spoken a word about this, their eyes were the line of communication to the other's heart.

The waiter and a gang of helpers brought out their dinner. The restaurant was so upscale that the waiter introduced the entree before revealing it, and although the couple already knew what they ordered, it was still amusing to them. The waiter removed the tin lid from Jade's plate, and she was stunned.

Assuming they had brought out the wrong food, she just went along with it. On her plate sat a thick cut of sirloin when she was expecting fish. The expression on her face was priceless. Devin looked at her from across the table, and he tried not to laugh. Her ignorance about a filet mignon was so cute and appealing to him.

She whispered across the table to him, "My order is wrong, but it's OK, I will still eat it."

Devin had ordered the same thing as her, and he knew that she knew, so he whispered back to her sarcastically, "My order is correct. It's just what I wanted, a filet mignon." Then he winked.

Her heart was in her stomach, and she felt the tips of her ears heating up. That was what happened when she got embarrassed. But Devin didn't mind, and after a while, she didn't either. The two began to partake in the dinner as the waiter poured wine.

Everything was perfect, and there was not another place in the world; either of them would rather be. Nothing else in the world mattered to them at this moment in time, but each other. There was complete silence while they ate.

Occasionally they would look up at each other and flash a smile, but they would say nothing major. They both indulged in the excellent food, not wishing to stop eating even to talk to one another. Before they knew it, both of them were nearing the end of their meals. Jade wiped her mouth with one of the fancy white napkins, took a sip from the glass of wine, and asked Devin, "So where do you see yourself in five years?"

Without hesitation, he responded. "I'm not that guy!"

"What guy?" Jade asked.

"You know, the one who says I'm going to do this by such and such time and before this happens. I'm a simple guy with a passion for how the body works and finding out what it takes to get maximum performance."

Devin was very serious when he spoke. It was sincere, and he meant it. It wasn't the answer Jade expected, but it was what she needed to hear. They got along very well and shared a common interest.

"Well, on a lighter note, when is your birthday?" From that question, until the end of the night, they conversed until they were ready to leave the restaurant. When they left, neither of them wanted to go home, and their body language said it. Jade was too shy to say anything, so she just twirled her thumbs. Devin felt her energy and noticed her fidgeting hands. Therefore he asked, "Do you want to go to the beach?"

Jade didn't hesitate. In fact, she nearly jumped out of her seat. Devin was surprised at her interest in him. His excitement wasn't as high as hers. He just didn't think she would be so into him. Devin pulled in to a vacant parking lot.

"I'm leaving my shoes in the car; I refuse to be embarrassed, trying to walk on the sand in heels."

Devin burst out laughing. "Now that would be a sight to see."

"What?" Jade asked.

"You breaking your ankles trying to keep your balance."

They laughed at each other. Devin took his shoes off as well and rolled his pants up. They walked the shore together, but there was an awkward distance between them. They just walked and talked for a while, about anything and everything. "Why are you so far away?" Devin asked.

"You're not one of my homeboys. You're my girlfriend." He added playfully.

Devin grabbed her waist and pulled her close to him. Naturally, she placed her arms around his neck. Now they were looking at each other right in the eyes.

The moon's glow illuminated the couple as it was darkness all around them. In her eyes, Devin saw fear; she was afraid to trust, afraid of love. In his eyes, Jade searched for warmth and protection. She wanted to see home. He pulled her closer until their lips touched.

Devin offered Jade something she had longed for ever since her grandmother had died. She wanted to matter to someone.

They stood on the shore under the moonlight and made out. Jade pulled him so close now she was squeezing him. The more intimate the kiss became, the more her juices began to flow. She was vulnerable, but not to the point of no return. She jerked away from him.

"What's wrong?" he asked.

"I don't want to jump the gun," she said. "Let's be patient with each other."

"I guess I gotta respect that," he added as he rolled his eyes. Jade was taken back by his gesture but tried to ignore it.

"OK, boyfriend, let's head back now."

Chapter 8

"Meeting at the diner on Madison Ave. 8 p.m., tonight."
Nicole sent a group text to the four girls who sparked an
interest in an exciting and erotic job opportunity. Before she
could put the phone down, she had a missed call from
Tyreke. She took a minute, contemplating whether she
should return his call or not.

"Nic, you working tonight?" Rachel's voice pierced
through the walls from the other room.

"Nah, I'm supposed to start my new job really soon."

"Girl, a Nine-to-Five don't take care of you like the pole."

Nicole didn't have a response to Rachel's sarcastic
remarks. All she could think about was convincing these
girls to join the 'team.' Her thoughts distracted her; she
forgot about calling Tyreke and instead texted Cloey.
"Thanks for picking me up the other night. The team is
almost together." She put her headphones on and laid on the
bed, staring at the ceiling fan until she slowly fell asleep.

It was 8:15, and none of the girls had arrived at the diner
yet. Nicole started to panic internally. The waitress had

asked her twice if she was ready to order. She just asked for another glass of orange juice. The restless girl was starting to feel doubtful. She thought all of this was a bad idea. But then the first girl walked into the diner.

"Hi, I'm Jessica, and this is my friend Tameka."

The girls' presence relieved Nicole. Her shoulders relaxed, and the other two girls could see her breathe heavily. She did not think anyone would show up, but importantly she did not know how she was going to explain that to Cloey.

"No, you girls are fine. It seems like everyone is running late."

The girls smiled back at her. Then Nicole had a great idea. She knew people liked to follow the crowd, so as an up and coming businesswoman, she would use this concept to her advantage.

She had initially planned to give the proposal to all the girls at once, but if one girl was not in agreement, her attitude might rub off on the others, and that wouldn't end well for Nicole. she thought. So her great idea was to ask these two girls before the others arrived. If they agreed, there would be three people down for the cause instead of Nicole by herself.

There is strength in numbers, indeed. If the girls did not agree, however, they could leave, and Nicole would be back at square one. She could still have her chances with the remaining girls without any negative influence of Jessica and Tameka's rejection.

Asking someone to participate in group sex was something new to Nicole, but she could not be afraid to fail. She convinced herself the worst that could happen was them not agreeing and thinking she was a weird person. She mentally amped herself up for this scenario and finally broke the silence at the table.

"So how would you both like to have sex with rich guys along with multiple other girls for about $2500 each time?" There followed a pause. Jessica and Tameka looked at one another and burst out laughing.

Then Tameka asked, "Is this a joke?" But Nicole was not laughing or even smiling.

"No, I'm serious." Nicole's seriousness made them laugh even harder. Trying to keep her composure, Nicole scoffed. She stood up from the table and was about to leave before Jessica said, "Wait, hold on." Jessica stared at Tameka, who seemed to nod slowly, continued.

"OK, to let you in on a secret, we are lesbians and have been trying to disguise ourselves as best friends since sophomore year in high school." Jessica's tone made the atmosphere intense and personal. "Lately, we have been trying to amp up our sex life, and the one thing we agreed on was threesomes with a male."

Jessica's confession was like music to Nicole's ears. It jazzed her up. "But we were both too shy because we are technically still virgins. So… We will need some experience first." Now, Nicole felt uneasy.

"And the multiple people idea is out of the question. The only two girls involved will be us two, no exceptions."

Without hesitation, Nicole agreed. "Sure!" It was not in the original plan, but it was good enough for starters.

"OK, great! Over the next week, we will stay in contact for STD testing and contracts," Nicole continued. She was trying to rush the process because she didn't want this attitude to affect the other girls who were now about an hour late.

"Perfect!" Jessica and Tameka said before standing up from the table, shaking hands and leaving the diner. Nicole was thrilled. She had doubted herself earlier when she could not believe she would have done anything like this. Her confidence shot through the roof. She felt invincible. She was amazed by herself, and it was for all the wrong reasons. Whenever she experienced a feeling of accomplishment, she always thought of Jade. She felt she should reach out to her. Without contestation, Nicole decided to send a text message.

She initially typed, "Hey, sis. I was thinking of you. I'm sorry about last time, I was wrong. Forgive me. I love you."

She read it once more before sending it. She was so proud and such an alpha-type personality. She deleted the message thinking it made her look weak. She deleted the entire thing. A tear formed in her eyes as she stared at a blank message box and a blinking cursor.

Before it could mature and roll down her cheek, she wiped it away, gathered her bag, and left.

The only things that could make Nicole emotional were her mother and Jade. She despised the fact they held that power over her. She had convinced herself she was emotionless. She believed nothing could hurt her if she didn't allow it to. The teary-eyed girl stood in front of the diner, a little puzzled. What should her next move be? She was momentarily distracted by thoughts of Jade. There was no sign of the other girls, but she wasn't at a complete loss either. She was level-headed and ready to go to Cloey's. She walked and stood at the bus stop waiting on the last bus, which would drop her off two blocks away from the club.

It wasn't long before the bus arrived. She usually paid the toll and sat towards the middle, no matter how many people would be on the bus. This time around, halfway through the ride, Nicole sensed a horrible feeling. Something made her stomach cringe. In spite of the restlessness, she ignored it altogether.

When Nicole was to get off the bus, she began to get extremely anxious. Her heart was pounding in her chest. The ride that usually takes about 10-15 minutes appeared to be taking hours. She had moved to sit at the front of the bus and even stood up. The bus stopped, and she got off. She felt as if her legs weren't moving fast enough. All she wanted was to tell Cloey the exciting news. The bus stop was around the corner from Cloey's, and during the walk between, she calmed herself down. Her palms were sweaty, and she was panting. By the time she reached Cloey's parking lot, she was at ease. Everything had slowed down to the regular, real-world pace. There wasn't a sense of urgency any longer. She had made her way inside the club and headed towards the staircase to Cloey's office. She was so focused and determined to get up the stairs she never once checked her surroundings. If she had done so, she would have noticed Rachel staring at her from across the room.

Rachel was entertaining a customer, but Nicole caught her eye as soon as she walked in. She could not pry herself away from staring at Nicole until she vanished upstairs. This made her boil on the inside. Rachel felt so upset her body temperature started to rise, making her forehead drip sweat. Rachel felt betrayed and was determined to find out what Nicole was up to. Nicole had reached Cloey's door, so anxious she didn't bother to knock and walked right in. It was evident that Cloey was anticipating her. She was sitting behind her desk with crossed arms, staring right at the door.

"I have two girls who are all-in, and they are lesbians, so it's all good," Nicole blurted it all out at once.

"Very well," Cloey said as well as nodding her head for reassurance. Nicole had expected a different reaction, but she was satisfied with the humble demeanor. Cloey could tell by her facial expression something was not right, so she asked, "Why are you looking like that? So hesitant."

Nicole replied, "I guess I expected a different reaction from you."

Cloey took a long second before responding, "Baby girl don't jump to conclusions, at least wait until they cut the check."

The concept seemed logical to Nicole, and if it hadn't, she wouldn't dare express her true feelings to Cloey. Her spirit was broken, but Cloey did not care. Nicole knew Cloey was right as well. She held her head down and took a glance at her phone for the time being. It was only 10:15. The last bus runs at eleven. Cloey knew Nicole's attitude had changed.

"The cup is half full, but it's not full. Keep your head up, and we will celebrate after the first job. Deal?" She was trying to boost Nicole's morale.

"Yea, I know. I'm going to leave before the last bus runs."

"Forget the bus. I will have my guy drive you home."

"OK, cool."

Cloey's attempt was unsuccessful, and Nicole had convinced herself she could not please her.

Cloey sent a text to her driver, then told Nicole, "Your ride is downstairs; we'll be in touch."

Nicole did not respond; just left the office, gently closing the door behind her. It was almost as if Nicole was having an out of body experience. She felt like she watched her body walk down the stairs, through the club, and out the door. There was a feeling of emptiness and unappreciation. By the time she was opening the car door, she felt like her real self again. Her day had been an emotional rollercoaster, and she just wanted to go home to sleep.

She opened the door, sat in the car, and a voice asked her, "So, are you going to tell me what's going on, or do I have to make you?"

Nicole was startled. She looked over and found Rachel. She had changed and was outside smoking before noticing Cloey's car was ready to leave before 10:30 p.m. Seeing Rachel relieved Nicole to a certain extent, but it was clear Rachel was serious. Nicole released a heavy sigh as an attempt to minimize the tension.

"Oh, girl. You scared me. I thought I was about to get mugged."

"No one is playing Nicole. I am serious. I saw you go up to Cloey's office, what do y'all have going on? 'Cause something ain't right!" Rachel demanded an explanation.

The girls made eye contact. Nicole realized Rachel was indeed as solemn as she warned she was. But she knew she couldn't tell her the truth. By the look in Rachel's eyes, Nicole knew she could no longer lie either.

"Well, see uhmm," Nicole was trying to stall, hoping she could come up with a quick lie to tell Rachel she would actually believe.

Rachel batted her eyes at her and puckered her lips out, anticipating Nicole's explanation. There was nothing Nicole could tell her but the truth.

"OK, Cloey and I have got this side thing going on," Nicole tried to be vague, but Rachel asked, "What side hustle?" Nicole dropped her head, partly in betrayal and partly in embarrassment.

"It's complicated." Before she could complete her thought, Rachel was already asking, "How complicated?"

There was a long pause before Rachel went off into a rant.

"Well, it is obvious this side hustle pays you more than the club because if not, you would not have quit. Number 2, since you're making more money, rent just went up to $300. And don't even think about moving out or not paying me my money because I will most definitely inform Cloey of your loose lips. Which brings me to number 3: your loyalty ain't shit. I got you this job, and you go behind my back and get a side hustle without letting me in. But it's cool, go ahead and get your extra cash and make sure I get mine as well."

Nicole was lost for words. She had no other choice but to agree to Rachel's terms.

"Hey driver, you can take us home now," Rachel said, then crossed her legs and smirked. Nicole was disgusted with herself and filled with regret. She just wanted this day to be over with.

Chapter 9

The next morning, Jade was walking to her car about to leave for school when she noticed Nicole sitting on the hood of her car. Caught by surprise, she slowed her pace as she approached. She had mixed feelings, given their last encounter. Although their previous altercation was the worst it had ever been, there was still no love lost from either of the girls. Jade walked to the driver's side of the car and unlocked the door, started the engine before reaching over to open the passenger side door and allowing Nicole to enter.

Nicole did not know how to initiate the conversation, where she would admit she was wrong and apologized. Jade was too strong. After completing anger management as a teenager, she had made a vow to herself ages ago that no one could get her upset only if she allowed them to. Whenever they have a misunderstanding, making up was a simple complication. There was a long awkward silence due to pride and lack of experience. Both of them wanted to apologize but could not find the words or strength to say it verbally. They drove around in awkward silence until Jade finally asked, "So, how have you been?" This is what typically happens. It was their own way of making up.

"Life's crazy." The tone Nicole spoke in, Jade could tell there was something wrong, but she also knew it was too soon to get emotional. Still trying to compose her toughness but not wanting to appear completely heartless, Jade replied, "I'm listening. Go on."

She was concerned about what was so 'crazy' in Nicole's life. But at the same time, she could not easily forget their last encounter. But they are sisters, Nicole was all Jade had in the world. The same went for Nicole, even though she did not know it. Nicole wanted to vent and tell her everything that was going on. She needed to release the tension, to feel better. She needed to exhale. She felt horrible about what she had been doing and thought how she could be so stupid to allow someone to manipulate her into manipulating others.

Before she could confess her guilt to Jade, the feeling she had at that moment was identical to the one she had before making the ultimate decision. As bad as she wanted to tell Jade, she just could not do it. There was resistance, invisible like a wall, and she could not break it down. So instead of being exact about things, she just replied, "It's crazy, you know? Trying to balance work, school, and leisure," smirking as she said 'leisure.'

Jade usually notices any uneasiness about Nicole, but because she was too focused, she missed the signs. Instead, she continued the conversation.

"Well, you know me, *no* fun and all work," she added emphasis on 'no.'

Nicole interrupted, "You mean to tell me no fun whatsoever?" she asked jokingly.

Jade had given in, "Well, a little fun, but I'm sure it wasn't as much fun as you've been having."

Nicole wasn't multi-tasking, so she could do what Jade couldn't and pick up on the little things.

"It's a guy, isn't it?" asked Nicole.

Jade paused and followed it up with a blush. "Yea, it is. He is a lot different from any of the other dudes I have ever met. He is everything, but at the same time, there is just something about him that I can't put my finger on."

Unaware and curious, Nicole asked, "Who is he?"

"Remember, Devin?"

"Devin!?" Nicole yelled out of shock.

"Of course I remember him, how could I forget?"

Nicole was not used to Jade indulging herself with one guy for any amount of time. Usually, she would have been with two or three different guys simultaneously while being with Devin already. Nicole was surprised yet happy for her sister.

"This is exciting. I knew a special guy would come along someday."

In the past, it was complicated for Nicole to have conversations with Jade about guys because she never had a real boyfriend. She never wanted Jade to feel uncomfortable or belittle her because she never had anyone to call her own until now.

"Well, what if I told you I have a guy as well?"

"Girl, there is always a guy with you. But sure, who is he?"

Nicole cut her eyes at Jade because she was the only one who would speak her mind without regarding how the other person received it.

"Well, his name is Tyreke, and he's cute and all, but he

just tries too hard."

Jade cocked her head and asked, "How does a guy try too hard?"

"I mean he's never in regular clothes, he always dresses like he sells insurance or is going to court," Nicole replied in a laughing manner.

"How was he dressed when y'all first met?"

"Like he sells insurance!" Nicole managed to get out before bursting into laughter.

Not knowing what to say, Jade replied, "Well, maybe he does sell insurance or something, and it requires him to dress the way he does."

Nicole was notorious for having sex with guys then later acting like she wants nothing to do with them. She mastered the art of seduction.

Jade entered the school premises and was running late for class.

"Hey, do you want to stick around campus until my class is over, and maybe we can grab food afterward?" Jade asked.

"Sure, I don't have plans today, anyways."

"OK, we'll just hang out in the student union, I'll be back in a couple of hours."

Jade went to class while Nicole went to the Student Union. Nicole was very familiar with the campus because she had been visiting her sister here since she was a sophomore at Tech, and she fit in with the student population. She had not been to the campus in a couple of months and did not know the Student Union now required a valid student I.D. for entrance. She approached the front counter and was about to be sent back, but one of the female basketball players recognized her as 'Jade's little sister,'

"It's cool, she's with us," she exclaimed. Nicole didn't know who she was, but she was grateful that she vouched for her.

She turned to the polite stranger, "Thank you."

"The pleasure is mine. By the way, I'm Ty, and you're Jade's little sister, correct?"

"Correct, I'm Nicole."

"Well, Nicole, what brings you to the Student Union when you're not a student?"

The way Ty asked was borderline interrogative, but more intimidating was the 6'2" teammate standing behind her like a security guard of some type.

Afraid at this point, she said, "Well, uhmm, I was passing the time until Jade got out of class."

"Why are you so scared, baby girl? It's OK. We don't bite, loosen up."

Ty could tell Nicole was uptight, but she relaxed after being told to.

She felt more comfortable. "What are y'all --?"

Before she could finish asking the question, the teammate had already gone towards the computers.

Ty responded, "I just came to chill," as she walked towards the lounge chairs. Nicole automatically followed her, staying a few paces behind as if they were connected by a short rope. The two had almost nothing in common. Nicole was very feminine, while Ty looked confused. Her hair was straight, pulled back into a ponytail, her nails were painted purple, but she was wearing a wife beater and oversized jeans. Nicole assumed she was a tomboy and left it at that. Not knowing exactly what to say, Nicole asked, "So how do you like Tech?"

Little did she know, she was about to open a can of worms she didn't want to deal with.

"Being a student-athlete is hard, especially when you have to depend on scholarships."

Confused, Nicole asked, "What do you mean? I thought if you play a sport, then the school pays for your tuition?"

"Yes, and no," replied Ty. "See, I have a partial athletic scholarship, and I have to maintain a 3.5 GPA to stay qualified for the academic scholarship."

"Oh, I see," Nicole answered. Ty then added, "I wish I could find a job that wouldn't interfere with basketball and could cover my tuition, and maybe it would be easier."

Nicole didn't want to reach out to any girls at Tech because she didn't want Jade to stumble onto what she was doing, but this opportunity was practically begging for grabs.

It indeed was too risky, because Ty knows Jade. There was too much room for error, but the opportunity was worth exploiting.

"I wish I had a sugar daddy, ain't nobody gonna know," Ty said eventually. Nicole's eyes stretched open as big as Ty's hooped earrings. she could feel this was the window she had been waiting for, so she pushed Ty further about it.

"Sugar daddies have money, and they can keep a secret," Ty added.

"Seriously? Nicole asked. This opportunity was almost too good to be true.

Ty said, "I wish I had a sugar daddy, ain't nobody gotta know, and sugar daddies got money and can keep a secret."

Ty replied, "So serious." She was looking Nicole right in the eyes with a straight face.

Nicole took a deep breath, "Well, what if I told you I'm involved in exactly what you are looking for?"

"You got a sugar daddy? Girl, put me on." Her comments stimulated Ty.

"Not a sugar daddy per se. But there is a lot more money and a lot more people involved."

"How much money and how many people?" Ty's curiosity was through the roof, and Nicole wasn't answering the questions fast enough.

"For you, anywhere between $800 and $1200, up to five people and as few as three."

Nicole's information was still too vague for Ty, "OK, what will I be doing exactly?"

"Parties!" Nicole replied.

"Stop playing, what type of parties pay that much and-" Ty had answered her question before she could finish asking it. She looked from left to right and then whispered, "You're into orgies?"

"I haven't done it yet, so I don't even know," Nicole answered.

"I've had a threesome before, so I imagine it can't be much different," Ty said. "I've only been with men, and I kissed a girl once in high school."

Nicole was about to say that all she has to do is kiss the girl. But Ty beat her to the punch. "I have wondered what it is like to be with a girl; my teammates talk about it all the time. But my parents wouldn't approve of me being in a lesbian relationship. Either way, I'm in."

Ty's utterance had Nicole in disbelief. Her job was done with little effort. Ty was the perfect kind of girl.

"Well, OK, hmmm, give me your number, and I will let you know something by the end of the week."

The two girls exchanged numbers, and their agreement was confirmed. They had nothing to talk about until Ty asked, "Nicole, do you know dude at the table reading the newspaper? His eyes have been glued to you since we sat down."

Ty bluntly pointed at the guy, and Nicole turned urgently to get a look at the man, neither of them was discreet about it. Once he realized the girls noticed him, he covered his face with the paper and ran to the nearest exit. Before Ty could tell Nicole to look back, all she could catch was his backside. The man was wearing basketball shorts and a bright orange shirt with white letters on the back that read, 'VOLUNTEER.'

Nicole said, "That's weird, I don't know many people who go to school here, especially no one who volunteers at the Student Union. If I did, I wouldn't have needed your help to get in." She added jokingly. As the two girls laughed, Ty noticed her teammate approaching. looking nervous. Ty nervously stated, "What we talked about stays between us."

Cunningly, Nicole replied, "What did we talk about?"

Ty smirked and said, "Exactly."

The oversized teammate plunged on the couch next to Ty and let out a huge sigh, "Ready to go?" Both the girls stood up. Ty told Nicole, "It was nice to meet you. Catch up with you later?" Nicole just smiled back and nodded. She left shortly after their departure when she received a text message from Jade urging her to meet by the car.

Chapter 10

Nicole got to the car, and she could instantly tell something was wrong. She was not her normal, optimistic self, and it was obvious in her tense body language. Once they were both inside, Jade drove in dead silence. Nicole, too, turned grim and confused. She rarely saw Jade emotional or display any type of vulnerability.

Finding Jade so crestfallen was out of the ordinary for her then. Thus, she habitually ignored her surroundings and pretended as if everything was normal. She fished out her earphones and escaped through music. Nicole lacked compassion. She had no regard for others' feelings, and it didn't matter if the distress was due to her or not. From the corner of her eye, she noticed a tear rolling down Jade's face.

Nicole felt herself grow terser. She didn't want to be there. She wished she could disappear, but she consoled herself with turning the volume fully loud. It was not enough. She wanted to run. She cringed in the passenger seat as she avoided her sister's literal cry for help. She observed her surroundings to try to look for one. There were only two restraints, a seatbelt, and a locked door, but she felt like she was trapped inside of a maximum-security prison cell with a life sentence. Nicole's neck was stiff, locked in a forward position as if it lacked flexibility. Jade sniffled and wiped her own tears. Feeling uneasy and trapped, Nicole didn't know what to say to her sister.

In fact, her mind was blank. The only thing she could think of was how to get out of this situation. Finally, Jade was the one to break the silence and relieve Nicole's anxiety with one simple question, "Are you hungry?" Jade's words released Nicole like a caterpillar in the final stages of metamorphosis. Jade noticed her shoulders visibly relax.

"Yes, I'm starving," Nicole replied. She plucked the earphones off and paused the music.

The two girls were sitting in a café, waiting for their order.

"How was the class?"

Nicole did not realize she was welcoming Jade to vent and putting herself back in an unwanted situation. From the look on Jade's face, it was apparent she did not want to talk about it. She knew avoiding the problem wasn't going to make matters any better. In those few seconds of silence,

Jade was struggling with the decision of whether or not she should tell Nicole. She was more inclined to keep it all bottled up like she always does. Jade often had battles within herself, a constant war between what she knows and what she feels. This time, she allowed the difficult but reasonable answer to be victorious and decided to open up to Nicole.

"Well, Devin went out of town a couple of weeks ago, and Tammy, one of my classmates, says she saw him with another woman." Jade's voice trembled.

Nicole stood up a little straighter. "Umm, how could that be when he was out of town?"

"I guess he never left and lied to me."

"You don't know that for sure, and who is this Tammy chick anyway?" Nicole asked.

"You know, Tammy. She switched majors my junior year. She's been at Tech for like six years," Jade responded sarcastically with an eye roll.

"Old bitch, she's like 30 and a professional student. She's gonna die and still be enrolled at Tech. She's lying, Jade." Nicole snapped back.

"Nah, she's not lying. I'm sure of that," Jade said, looking down and fiddling with her bag.

"How are you so su-" Before Nicole could finish asking the question, Jade had already opened her phone, preparing to show her the pictures supporting Tammy's accusations. Jade passed the phone to Nicole so she could see it as well. Nicole stared at the phone for a long time without even blinking her eyes. She was so still Jade could not even tell if she was breathing. Concerned, she nudged her sister, and she asked, "Are you OK?"

Nicole was shell-shocked, but she managed to say something finally, "This is foul." She then added, "I really don't even know what to say. I thought he was different."

Nicole's disbelief didn't make Jade feel any better. Jade broke into tears, and she could not control them. Devin's actions crushed her heart. She thought she had known pain considering her past from her "fly by night" encounters.

This pain was a lot different. She never addressed her issues as open as she was doing today.She never had a reason to. All the guys would eventually fade away, physically, and emotionally. But Devin was different and unique. Other than the pictures, Jade never had a reason to question his character. As she reminisced about the pleasant times they shared, she was trying to convince herself it wasn't true. Jade's mind raced about their short-lived relationship, and she could not recall anything that would make her think there was another woman. She thought he was too good to be true. She finally found a flaw.

"So, what are you gonna do?" Nicole broke her sister's stream of thought.

"Nothing."

Jade despised confrontation. Her calm response did not come as a shock to Nicole.

Suddenly, she was at peace. Her tears stopped flowing, and she even gave a nonchalant shoulder shrug. Nicole was infuriated at this point.

"No! No, you're not. You better give Devin the full clip, I'm talking show him the pictures and everything. If anything has ever made you think twice about him, this is your time to bring it up."

At this point, Jade did not know what she was going to do. Her mind raced uncontrollably, and her eyes were distant. She had never been in a real relationship before, let alone had a real break up. This was her first time dealing with such a thing. Yet again, she was at a crossroads with the war raging against her heart and her brain. Her heart and emotions were in so deep. She did not even care if he had another woman on the side. It didn't matter to her. What mattered to her was how he treated her better than any guy she had ever been with. Even if there was someone else, when they were together was she felt like she was his only one.

"I don't care if there was someone else," she said to Nicole after a minute.

When she heard herself say these words, her mindset immediately changed. It gave her a feeling of submission like she was belittling herself. She felt unworthy and weak. Before Nicole even had a chance to respond, Jade started to think aloud.

"What am I doing, what did I just say?" She stared out the window, held her head, and began to rant as if she was speaking to a crowd of people. "Never allow anyone to have such power over you that you start to alter your morals and question your self-worth. You should always be your

number one supporter. Earn everything you have, so no one can have the satisfaction to say you owe them anything." Jade shook her head and scowled her face.

Nicole was confused. She wasn't sure if Jade was still talking about Devin anymore, let alone talking to her. She wanted to say something but did not know what point to address. As she searched for the right words to agree with Jade, she received a message.

"First gig this weekend, get your girls together." It was from Cloey.

Now, Nicole's thought process was in knots. She was uncertain about how to respond to Jade and rescue her from her daze, for she had a list of questions to ask Cloey as well.

She whispered to herself, "One thing at a time." She responded to Cloey first. "We will talk particulars later."

Because her mind got boggled, her response to Jade was generic and lacked sincerity.

"You just have to do what you gotta do and what's best for you, Jade."

Without hesitation, Jade said, "You already know what I'm doing." She instantly added. "I'm not even hungry anymore, ready to go?"

"Yes, I am."

They left the cafe leaving behind ten dollars on the table. As they were exiting the building, Nicole already started attending to her work.

She sent out a mass text message to all of her girls, "Gig this weekend! Are you available?"

Before reaching the car, Jade asked Nicole, "If you don't mind, can you take the bus?"

Nicole didn't mind because she was going to Cloey's, and she certainly didn't want Jade to drop her off there.

"Yes, it's fine."

"OK perfect, I will talk to you later," Jade said before getting into her car.

Nicole just nodded and walked to the bus stop across the street. Jade sat in her car, put on her seatbelt, but before starting the car, she sent a message to Devin, "Hey, can I come over?"

She then started the engine and proceeded to his apartment. A million thoughts rushed through Jade's mind. What was she gonna say? How would she say it?

She even questioned herself, "How could I have been so blind? No guy is ever nice. I should've known better. I should have seen it coming." By this time, she had driven four blocks and stopped at a traffic light. While waiting for the light to turn, she checked her phone for a reply from Devin, but there was none.

This only fueled her anger more and gave her the ammunition for when she would confront him. She did not realize how angry she was until the light turned green, and she smashed the gas as hard as she could, earning a screeching *eeeeeekh* from her car tires. She didn't want to draw attention, so she tried to maintain the speed limit on her way to Devin's.

Her blood was still boiling. She was furious. Her heart was pounding with negativity, and deception occupied her thoughts. She considered all of the possibilities of why he would not respond to her. She could not think of one explanation that would justify him not returning her text messages. The fact that this was the first time Devin didn't respond made matters worse. Another traffic light around the corner stopped her near Devin's apartment building. She checked her phone one last time, and still, there was nothing. Now, she concluded he was purposely, not responding. Jade assumed that he was with another woman at his apartment. She was preparing herself to catch him red-handed.

The light indicated the 'go,' and she sped off again, whipping around the corner and parking in the lot in front of Devin's building. He lived on the second floor, so she ran up a flight of stairs, skipping every other step. She rang the doorbell, panting, but he couldn't answer fast enough before she started banging on the door.

In between her knocking, she could hear him yell through the door, "Hold on, I'm coming." The sound of his voice gave her a slight relief because it meant he was in the apartment, and at least safe, and her emotional rollercoaster would mean something and not be pointless.

Devin opened the door with a bath towel wrapped around his waist. He immediately asked, "What's wrong?" He was under the assumption there was an emergency. Jade was in a rage, and Devin answering the door in a bath towel was all the evidence she needed.

She pushed him back into his apartment and demanded to know, "Where is she?"

Dumbfounded, Devin asked, "Where is who?"

Jade was already rummaging his place, looking behind couches, in closets, behind doors. She thoroughly checked every room, not leaving behind one inch. On her rant down the hallway to double-check the living room, he grabbed her and yelled, "What are you doing, and who are you looking for?"

She answered, looking him straight in the eyes, "I'm looking for the girl you were with when you were so-called out of town!"

Now Devin was extremely confused and grew frustrated. Unsure of where to begin, Jade simply showed him the pictures which she had gotten from Tammy.

Devin looked at the first picture, and before even looking at the others, he asked, "Where did you get these from?"

The look in his eyes was something vicious. Jade felt afraid, but her fear did not stop her from standing her ground.

"Don't worry about where I got them from, just know I have them now."

Devin stared her down, then let out an exaggerated sigh of relief and then, to Jade's surprise, smirked. He sat on the couch and put his feet on the coffee table and crossed his arms, finally asking, "So, what now?"

Jade had not thought that far into her dramatic showcase. She allowed her emotions to deceive her into thinking he was with another woman and that she would catch them together at his apartment. She held her head down, searching for something clever to respond with, but found nothing. As she slowly lifted her head, he had already begun to speak.

"So, you thought I was cheating on you with the woman in the picture?" He raised his eyebrows as he said it. Jade was about to answer his question before he interrupted her, "And you thought she was here and you were going to catch us in the ac-"

Devin started laughing before completing the question. His sarcasm made Jade feel two feet tall, but Devin continued to laugh. Jade was embarrassed and too ashamed. She dropped her head again and whispered, "I'm sorry."

He patted on the couch next to him. "Come here and let me see the picture again."

Jade was hesitant for a moment, but she sat on the couch next to him and showed him the pictures. He pulled her closer to him and put his arm around her neck and shoulders, embracing her.

"This woman is Yolanda. She is a colleague, and this was taken at a luncheon last year."

"But did you have sex with her?" Jade asked.

"Yolanda and I have known each other for quite some time because we work in the same field. A while ago, we tried to be more than just colleagues and lasted for all of four days. We got drunk, one thing led to another, and sex got mistaken for feelings. But it's nothing now."

"So what happened, how come you guys didn't work out?"

"Because there was nothing to work out. And I'm done with this conversation."

"Wait, wait! One last question. Do you see her often? I mean, since y'all do work in the same field."

Before answering, Devin grabbed Jade's hand, getting her full attention. "I have not seen nor talked to this woman in over six months. It doesn't even matter if I do, because the only woman I'm looking for is the one I love."

"Who do you love?" she asked, tentative and with her heart pounding.

"You!"

Before even realizing it, she shot back, "I love you too."

Devin looked shocked as the words rolled off of Jade's lips and that too so swiftly. Realizing what she said, he grabbed her face, pulled her in, and started kissing her passionately.

Chapter 11

Nicole got off the bus around the corner from Cloey's. Unlike previously, she wasn't as nervous. Although the walk from the bus stop to the club was not far, it always used to be a weird feeling for Nicole. Initially, she couldn't figure Cloey out, but that was then, and this is now. She was aware that their relationship was transactional and felt content with it.

The only uneasy feeling she had was the feeling that she was being followed. It perplexed Nicole because it was still fairly early at night. She looked over her shoulder frequently, but more times than not, she saw the same thing, an empty, poorly lit street.

After what seemed like forever, she finally reached the parking lot of the club. She glanced behind her once more before entering the club. She could've sworn she saw the top of someone head duck down behind a car. She furrowed her brow then shrugged, convincing herself it was only her imagination laying tricks on her. She went inside the club to the sound of booming music. Nicole walked in just when Rachel was performing.

It was already a challenge for Rachel to hold a crowd's attention for the duration of her performance, and when a fully dressed Nicole walked through the room, the task became more difficult. Nicole did not even entertain the attention; in fact, she barely noticed anyone. She had tunnel vision for Cloey's office. Rachel, on the other hand, most definitely noticed. As soon as Nicole walked by the dance floor, more than half of the room's heads shifted in her direction.

This made Rachel furious yet jealous without wanting to. She was never intimidated by Nicole because she had confidence in herself. This was the first time throughout their friendship that Rachel compared herself to Nicole. It made her feel ugly and disgusted with herself. The feeling was so intense, she cut her performance short and ran into the dressing room.

Cool, calm and collected, Nicole knocked on Cloey's door and immediately received an invitation. "Come in." Once inside the room, Cloey instructed Nicole to take a seat. In typical Cloey fashion, she used her fearful tactics by taking her time and using her eyes as daggers to pierce through Nicole's soul. But Nicole overcame the tension.

With a smile on her face and a casual sweeping glance, she felt unbothered by Cloey's scare tactics. As usual, there was a long silence before either of them said anything. Usually, Cloey would do all the talking, but this time Nicole took charge.

"So, what's the deal with this first job?"

Cloey was shocked because Nicole initiated the conversation just when she was about to speak. "Well," she said squinting at Nicole, "It's a higher roller"

"How much and how many girls?" Nicole interrupted Cloey with a steadfast response. Cloey did not get upset; she only continued.

"Two girls. $2000 per girl."

Processing the price and nodding her head, Nicole asked, "OK, I got two girls, how much in it for me?" Her intentions were for the lesbian couple Jessica and Tameka to take the first job.

In the middle of her brainstorming, Cloey said, "See here's the thing," leaning forward and meeting her eyes, she said, "He has requested you."

Nicole got shocked upon hearing that. She immediately snapped from businesswoman to client, her boldness diminishing instantly.

She cleared her throat and tried not to show her alarm any further. She asked, "If I'm in the party, how much would it be?"

"Well, it is unfair to the other girl because y'all will be doing the same thing, but I will keep my word, so three grand."

"Five!"

Cloey yelled back, "3500."

Nicole gained her confidence back and insisted, "Four thousand, nothing lower. Take it or leave it." She gripped the hands of her chair, ready to leave.

"Wow, I'm impressed," Cloey settled back into her chair and folded her arms. She was smiling and was impressed by Nicole's negotiating skills. "I'm creating a lil warrior, ain't I?" Cloey was being sarcastic and was manipulating her into thinking Nicole had won.

"Nah, I've been a warrior since forever," Nicole jabbed back.

"Yeah, I know," Cloey cut it short. "I haven't gotten any particulars for you yet. Just be ready at any time over the next 3 to 4 days."

Nicole stood up from the chair, nodded, and left Cloey's office feeling self-satisfied. As she was walking down the stairs to the club area, she sent a text message to Ty, "We're hot, on call for 3-4 days. $2K payout."

Nicole was making her way across the club, and before she made it to the door, her phone rang. "No problem, I'm down." It was Ty.

She smiled at her cell phone, but a firm grip on her hand disturbed her brief moment of joy. She looked right into the interrupter's eyes and did not even recognize him at first. He was a light-skinned guy with a black t-shirt, sweatpants and a baseball cap on.

"Tyreke?" She asked, confused, and aggravated.

"Have you been avoiding me?" He was fuming.

She had not recognized him because she had never seen him dressed down before. He was always in business casual attire.

"No I haven't been avoiding you, I've just been busy. I told you about that."

"I must be crazy then," Tyreke spat. "Because you don't even work at the club anymore, yet you're always here." And then, in an instant, his whole demeanor changed. "So, where have you been? I miss you, and I never see you anymore."

Nicole had seen this look before. Not from Tyreke, but every other guy from her past after they fell for her following a passionate night of ecstasy. Nicole had been through this cycle so many times. It had become predictable.

At this point, she didn't care, not that she ever did in the first place. She had been trying to put him down in a nice way, but he never got the hint. The approach she was about to take would expedite the "break up" process, at least that's what she assumed.

In the past, she would string the guy along with no intentions of ever dating. But she would allow them to profess their love for her and buy her gifts before she gave them the ultimatum. Having graduated high school, Nicole now thought of herself as a grown woman who didn't have time to play the "cat and mouse" game. Besides, she was about to be making more money than she ever had, so she didn't need Tyreke's gifts and such.

"Listen, Tyreke. We will never be an item. I will never date you. It was fun for a while, whatever "it" was. The sex, though, was awful, and I just can't see myself with a guy like you."

She did not even remove her eyes from his until she completed her dialogue. She just let it all out at once without sugarcoating or watering it down. She intended to hurt his feelings and bruise his ego so he wouldn't want anything to do with her. After ripping his heart out, she didn't even stick around to see his reaction. She said what she had to say with hopes he would leave her alone and finally stepped out of the club.

Tyreke stood right there at his spot with his pride and dignity in each pocket, and his ego on the floor. His mouth was wide open, his eyebrows knit. He did not want to believe what just happened. He could have melted standing right there in the middle of the club. He swept a damp palm over his face and thought that all he could do now was go to the bar and drink the hurt away. Watching from across the room while entertaining a client, Rachel's mind raced and rambled, trying to figure out exactly what just transpired between the two. Rachel was a loose cannon, and she had no idea who this guy was, but she was still very anxious to know.

Because she wasn't certain of him, she watching him indulged in shot after shot and beer after beer from a distance. She devised a plan to take advantage of his vulnerability. After watching her prey for about an hour and a half and watching him turn down private dances one after the other, she figured out the perfect time to attack. She approached him from his blindside and sat next to him at the bar. He was ordering another round.

"Hey there, handsome."

He did not even glance at her. "Like I told the last girl and the one before her and the others before her too, I don't want a dance or anything you have to offer," Tyreke snapped at Rachel in a voice made hoarse from all the alcohol.

"Are you sure I don't have anything to offer?" Rachel traced the tip of her finger over the ring of an empty glass. She just needed him to say anything she could capitalize on.

"I already told you, lady, there is nothing you can do for me. What I want, nobody can give me but one girl."

That was it. That was all she needed.

"If I can't do it for you, then who can? I mean, what if I have the resources to get to the one?" she asked craftily.

"Excuse me?" He asked, finally looking at her with intoxicated eyes. He had given her the inch she was searching for, but she was about to take a mile.

"You're getting drunk at a strip club and don't want any attention from any of the girls, either you just got dumped, or you're gay."

"I'm not gay." He said after processing her comment for a minute.

"So, who was she?' Rachel already knew the answer to most of the questions she would ask, but not all of them. She wanted to appear as a random girl who has a mutual associate.

"Her name is Nicole."

"Nicole, who used to work here?" Rachel feigned a surprised look.

"You know her?" Tyreke asked in desperation.

"I mean, I know her, but I don't *know* her." Rachel lied.

"Well, I mean, can you tell me what she has been doing? She's never here at work but says she always busy."

Rachel's curiosity increased. "Nah, she doesn't work here anymore, and I don't know what she's doing." That was the first truthful thing Rachel had told Tyreke. She added, "Whatever she's involved in, there's some money in it."

"Money?" Tyreke questioned. "She doesn't have to worry about no damn money. I was going to take care of her." He slammed at the table, the drunkenness settling in him. "All I wanted from her was to be mine!"

Now Rachel was spiking with curiosity regarding what was going on with Nicole and Cloey. After their confrontation, she let it go because of their new rental agreement, but this was about something more than money. Rachel was constantly thinking, and Tyreke was constantly talking. She could still hear fragments of what he was saying but nothing that she could use until he said, "I will pay you."

"Huh? What?"

"If you can find out what she's doing, if it's something about another man, whatever it is, I will pay you for it." The desperation in his voice was as strong as the stench of alcohol from his mouth.

"How much?"

"How much you want?"

"Ten grand... upfront."

He was taken aback by that. "Girl, you must have lost your mind. I don't even know your name, and you want me to give you $10,000 so that you dupe me and run off into the sunset."

Even though all the signs had shown it, Tyreke wasn't as drunk as Rachel thought he was. But she knew his judgment was impaired, and she wasn't walking away from him empty-handed.

"Well, if that's your choice," she readied herself to walk away. "You lose out on the girl of your dreams just because you don't wanna spend a lousy ten grand."

"Alright, OK." That was like music to Rachel's ears. "I will give you five now and five later, but you got two weeks to bring me something back, or you don't get the other five."

"OK, deal." Rachel agreed and shook on it.

"I will bring you the check tomorrow." He quickly gulped his remaining drink and tottered out of the club.

Rachel had been excited but now was motivated about finding out what Cloey and Nicole were up to. She wanted to start immediately. Her curiosity was getting the best of her, and the promised incentive from Tyreke only amplified her drive.

After he left the club, Rachel sat at the bar, strategizing a plan to acquire the info she needed from Nicole. After half an hour of contemplating when nothing concrete came to her, she decided to call it a night.

What she thought would be the end of the night became more. When she arrived home, Nicole was still up. Rachel took this as the perfect opportunity to start investigating for Tyreke.

Rachel sat on the living room sofa next to Nicole and asked, "Hey there, you. How's it been going on?"

From her unusual concern, Nicole knew something was up. She recognized this but continued to answer as vaguely as before.

"You know, it's been going, nothing too serious."

Rachel saw Nicole had caught on. She decided to ease into the situation first instead.

"So, how's the new job?"

Nicole delayed her response partially in disbelief and partially because she was trying to think of a clever comeback. But she had nothing. Instead of responding, she felt determined to ignore her. Rachel was silently waiting for an answer. Nicole answered with picking up the remote control and changing the television channel. Bullying would not work on Nicole, so Rachel tried to empathize and use the sincerity of their friendship for leverage.

"You remember my sweet sixteen/baby shower/sleepover party?" Nicole smirked.

"How could I forget? You were seven months pregnant trying to have a birthday party, and everyone bought gifts for your baby instead of you." Rachel gleamed. "Then, you got so emotional when it was time to leave; everybody felt sorry and had to stay for you." Both the girls burst into laughter as they reminisced on the day.

"Yeah, even though the day was wild and unpredictable, it was one of the better days of my life so far."

The tension in the room was starting to ease, and Nicole let her guard down.

"I remember after you had the baby and finally came back to school, everybody was talking trash, and I slammed Bethany Mitchell's head into the locker for spreading the rumor that you didn't know who your baby's father was," she giggled to herself. "To this day, my mom doesn't know I was suspended from school."

"No way." Rachel burst out into another bout of a laugh, and Nicole followed. Then after they recovered, Rachel decided to seize the opportunity.

"I remember when we first met in junior high. We have been friends ever since, right. We were so close. What happened then? We used to tell each other everything."

Rachel was using an emotional trap to dive into Nicole's secrets. Her tactics worked, and it made Nicole open up. Nicole had felt bottled up and in need of venting to someone about the work she now did. It wasn't that she felt it was immoral, because she had already convinced herself she was only doing it temporarily until she saved up enough money to get away. There was so much going on. She needed to get something off her chest to relieve the stress.

"I gotta… I gotta get outta this town, Rachel. I want to go somewhere I've never been and just stay there."

"Somewhere, like where exactly?" Rachel sat up straighter.

"I don't know, I just want to up and leave."

"Oh. And when do you plan on leaving?"

"Once I save up enough money, I guess."

Rachel had opened the door to the vault and suddenly was back in attack mode.

"Wait, how much money do you plan on saving? And how fast are you gonna get it? How much are you even making at this new job, Nicole?"

Rachel realized she had gotten carried away just when Nicole realized she had been manipulating her. She gave her friend a look of disgust that changed to hurt. Nicole felt the heat gather behind her eyes while Rachel, unpredictably, found a guilt welling inside of her. Nicole shook her head as a tear finally rolled down her cheek, "I can't believe you... Why did you do that? I trusted you, and you just planned to use my shit against me?! I knew something was not right about you coming in and pretending to care about me. Shit."

Nicole got up and stomped away from Rachel into her bedroom. Rachel sat on the sofa, trying to put together what just happened. She felt terrible for doing what she did, but it had been too late then.

Their friendship would never be the same now, and she knew it.

Chapter 12

The next morning, Nicole woke up before the sunrise. She threw some clothes in a bag and left for Jade's apartment. She took her time getting there because she didn't want Jade to suspect anything about the night before with Rachel.

After three tedious hours, she finally knocked on Jade's door. She was already awake and preparing to go to campus for her morning class. The girls didn't say much to each other. They didn't really need to. Nicole sat on the sofa and watched television; Jade continued to get dressed. In the car, on the ride to campus, Nicole initiated the conversation.

"How did things go with Devin?"

Jade thought for a minute before she answered. She didn't want to let Nicole know she had given into him, although she was confused about what to believe. She tried to keep it vague and short as possible.

"We argued for a long ass time then had make-up sex."

"How was the make-up sex?" Now Nicole had a smirk on her face.

Jade smiled to herself and responded, "The best I've ever had."

Nicole laughed out loud and added, "Don't go falling for dick, if you want him to respect you and see if he really cares, you gotta even the playing grounds."

"Now, Nic. You know that ain't my style."

"Girl, forget your style, sometimes you gotta treat these dudes how they treat you. You gotta show them you want them, not need them. That's when they appreciate you more."

Although Jade believed in being faithful in her relationship no matter what Devin did, she was contemplating taking Nicole's advice and trying something different. Especially since she hadn't had a successful relationship where she got her own way in twenty-two years of living.

They headed towards the training room once they were on campus. Jade had to prepare the room for the athletes as they were to come in later. Nicole went to so many meets and events with Jade, she knew the preparation routine as well as anyone on their staff. They worked together while they swayed to the music.

The radio was playing. Jade and Nicole were moving to the beat around the room and singing the lyrics as they tossed ACE bandage and athletic tape to one another. Their energy was infectious, so much so that when the other staff members entered the room, they picked up dancing and singing too. The potency of their vibe filled the room with positive energy; it came alive. There was laughter, and there was dance and joy too. What started out as an impromptu duet, grew into a group effort. About an hour before the athletes usually began to pour in, the athletic director stuck his head in through the door and motioned for Jade to meet him outside. She did as directed.

"Hey, Dr. Greene, are we too loud?" She asked, now out of breath and covered in sweat. Jade assumed she was in trouble. She continued, "I can tone it down a little bit if you wish."

To her surprise, the director had the opposite reaction. "No, I love what you have going on in there. We, here at Tech, will definitely miss this energy once you've graduated and moved on."

Jade could not resist blushing as Dr. Greene complimented her.

"Well, what's going on?" She asked.

"First, I would like to apologize for not informing you prior, but because of the great job you have done here the past couple of years, I submitted your name and resumed to attend an all-inclusive seminar in Jamaica for young trainers. There will be youngsters such as yourself there; it's an experience of a lifetime. I think you'll have fun."

Jade's eyes grew bigger, as he explained.

"You were selected amongst ten other trainers to attend. At the seminar, you will compete against the others in an indirect perspective."

Now, Jade was confused.

"What do you mean by compete?"

"They choose the best of the ten prospects after the seminar, basing their decision on their strengths/weaknesses, personality, and resilience in regards to adversity."

Still, a bit puzzled, "What's the position?"

Dr. Greene took a deep breath, "US Olympic Track and

Field trainer."

Jade felt her heart sink into her stomach, she managed to utter, "Don't play with me, are you serious?"

"Yes, I am serious. And it gets better." He smiled, amused at every reaction, his words were spurring. "The job is in Los Angeles. I know one of the guys on the decision board, and he informed me, collectively, that the board was most impressed with you."

Jade whispered to herself, "Los Angeles?" Her excited grin faded to a look of shock. Dr. Green presented her with an opportunity of a lifetime, but she was skeptical about it due to its location. She was grateful that he believed in her and was appreciative of him submitting her information. How could she disappoint him after all he did? She managed a smile and hugged him and then returned to the training room with the others.

The room was filled with the same contagious positivity. However, Nicole, consumed by her cellphone, did not look like the same joyous person. She was feeling numb, thinking about the upcoming evening.

"Tonight's the night," Nicole read a text message from Cloey to herself. Reacting immediately, she texted Ty the same message. "Tonight is the night." Before Nicole could ask, Cloey had already sent a second text message informing her of the time and location. Instead of giving Ty so many details, she just told her to be ready after the track meet.

For the duration of the track meet, neither Jade nor Nicole was mentally there. They both were so caught up in their own issues; they didn't even notice each other. Time was going by faster than either of them wanted to. Jade didn't know how to tell Nicole about her life-changing opportunity, let alone +Devin.

She wished she could avoid the conversation, but she knew that was not an option, and she had to tell her both the things tonight. Nicole, on the other hand, had no intention of ever telling Jade about her life-changing experiments. She did, however, dreaded having to do it. Unknowingly they both had the same wish to fast forward to the next morning.

Before either of the girls realized, the track meet was over, and all they had left to do was clean the training room. Just as they were leaving the building, Nicole received a text message from Ty, "In the parking lot." She locked her phone.

There was no turning back from this point. With every opportunity she had had to quit, she couldn't muster up the courage. In the middle of Nicole contemplating the exact moment to quit, Jade bulleted her story out in a single breath.

"I'm going to Jamaica next week for a seminar to get a job in LA as an Olympic trainer, but I technically already have the job."

She was surprised how much of a relief it was actually to tell Nicole, who was greatly taken aback.

"Whoa, slow down there. You're going to the Olympics in Jamaica? Next week? What?" Nicole was baffled.

"No, silly! I'm going to Jamaica next week for a seminar."

"OK, that's great."

"They are offering me a job as an Olympics trainer." Jade relished how it felt, saying it out loud.

"Why you gotta go to Jamaica for a job offer you already know about right now?"

"Well, that's where it gets complicated, the seminar is a front. I basically already have the job because I'm the most qualified. I have to present myself now, show that I'm likable."

"So what's the problem? I don't get it. Take your ass to Jamaica, have the time of your life. Take the damn job offer."

"The job is in LA."

"So what? What's left here for you... NOTHING... you're trippin'."

"But Devin's here."

"Didn't he cheat on you?"

"I don't know that for sure."

Nicole paused for a beat. Then said, "Female intuition is never wrong."

"Hell, if I were you, I would get me one of them fine specimens of a man, take him to paradise, come back, tell Devin and break up with his lying ass."

Jade looked at her speechless. Although she was still uncertain, she didn't want to assume and be wrong; therefore, she acted as if it never happened. She was slightly relieved she told Nicole, but that was only half the battle because she didn't know how Devin would react. By the time they reached Jade's car, Ty was already there.

"Hey y'all, what's going on?"

Jade was surprised to see Ty there. Nicole was surprised at how excited she was.

"What are you doing here, are you OK?" Jade automatically assumed she was in trouble.

Before Ty could answer, Nicole intervened, "She's staying the night at my place. She's gotta teach Rachel and me how to cook mac and cheese from scratch."

All three girls were confused by Nicole's response; it showed on all their faces. Everyone knew that was a lie but refused to address it.

"My bad, sis. I was supposed to tell you, but it slipped my mind."

Jade nodded. She knew Nicole had too much going on in her own life to focus on other suspicions. They all sat in the car for an awkward and silent ride.

Nicole broke the silence. "You can take us to the grocery store to get all the ingredients we need." It earned her the dirtiest of looks from Jade. Feeling vulnerable and meek,

Nicole used sarcasm as her defense mechanism. She added, "And you don't have to wait. I don't want to delay you telling Devin the big news."

Jade stopped the car with a screech and insisted Nicole got out. The already awkward air shifted further. Nicole leaving meant Ty getting out too. Jade apologized to Ty but had no remorse for Nicole. Nicole just laughed and got out of the car. Before slamming the door, she said, "You're just blinded by sex, you know. That man is playing you."

Jade ignored the first statement, but the second sentence pierced her deep. She was never great at comebacks, so she just didn't say anything at all; just put the car in gear and sped off, leaving the girls on the roadside. Nicole was already on her cell phone, calling Cloey.

"Yea, we on Grant, almost at 179th." She hung up the phone.

"Our ride is on the way."

"You and Jade always argue?" Ty asked. She had lost her enthusiasm when she was kicked out of the car and did not want to do the gig with a bad vibe.

"Yea, we fall out sometimes, but you know… sister stuff." Nicole responded.

"Are you good for what we are about to do?" Ty asked out of concern.

"I'm good, but I'm about to get right as soon as this ride comes."

Ty was uncertain about what 'getting right' was. But not risking being too inquisitive, she sat patiently because she would eventually find out. Ty was expecting a cab or even just a regular car, but she was caught off guard when a limousine pulled up to get them. Cloey was already in the backseat. As soon as Nicole sat, the vehicle began to accelerate. Cloey asked, "You sure?"

"I had a long day, yes, I am sure." Her hand was on her head.

Cloey was still hesitant. Nicole barked back, "You trying to get this money, right?"

"Say no more." Cloey opened up a compartment and grabbed a shoebox, and handed it to Nicole. She flipped the top off and tossed a bag filled with a white substance onto the shoebox top. Then she took her identification card and began to chop the white substance, separating it into lines. She grabbed a twenty-dollar bill and rolled it up. Finally, she stuffed one end of the rolled bill into her nostrils and snorted a line of the white substance up her nose. With one more line left on the shoebox top, Nicole offered it to Ty, "Are you going to get right?"

"Ye-yea, bu-bu-but not like that." Ty stuttered. Cloey offered Ty a couple of shots from the mini-fridge.

"Good thing, more for me." Nicole snorted the second line. She leaned her head back and allowed the drugs to 'get her right.' It always hit her hard at first, but after the first ten minutes, the feeling of invincibility would settle in. As Ty took her shots and Nicole got right, Cloey explained the procedures of what was about to take place.

"OK, we are going to get a hotel room. You two will already be in the room before the client arrives. I suggest starting with foreplay before he comes in. This particular client wants to fulfill a fantasy of walking in on two girls making love, and they invite him to join."

Both Ty and Nicole listened intently, absorbing everything Cloey was saying.

"It's only eight right now. He won't be there until ten at the earliest. So, take a shower, freshen up, and make the room yours. I will give him the key so he will not knock. But for it to go well, you HAVE to be already engaged in sex."

At this point, Nicole was 'right,' and she sniffed and said, "Hell yea, let's do this." She then pulled Ty's face to hers and started making out. Both the girls were intoxicated and were ready to have fun. Ty moaned and started breaking out of her shell. She yelled to the driver, "turn up the radio. We're trying to party." He did so, and the girls went wild.

Once at the hotel, Cloey went inside the lobby to get a room and make sure the girls were ready. By the time Cloey returned to the limousine, things had heated up by degrees. Nicole was the aggressor; she had taken off Ty's top and was kissing on her cleavage and stomach.

"Whoa, whoa, whoa, save that for a lil bit later, would ya."

Cloey managed to get both the girls from the vehicle and up to three flights of stairs into the room. She didn't leave the room until about 9:20, ensuring that both girls showered. Ty insisted Cloey bring the bottle of liquor before she left, which she did. Cloey reminded the girls she would be back to get them the next morning by 10 a.m. Immediately after Cloey left, both girls took two shots, all the while staring at each other. Both of their hormones were raging out of control. Although Nicole had been with a girl before and Ty hadn't, that did not stop Ty from enjoying the experience.

Nicole was lying across the bed. Ty walked up to her and grabbed each of Nicole's ankles. She spread her legs apart and pulled her body towards her simultaneously. Ty anxiously tried to take Nicole's top off. She liked Ty's dominance, and she wanted it to last. Nicole grabbed Ty's hips and pulled them close to her pelvis. The narrow space between them prevented Ty from rushing the act and instead calmed her down, forcing her to take her time. This was her first encounter with a girl, and although it was strictly business, it was as if they were actual lovers.

They had managed time very well unknowingly. By the time the client entered the room, the girls had on cue become completely nude. They were so engrossed that they didn't even notice his presence. He himself had to make his way between them. For the duration of the sexual encounter, neither of them made eye contact with the client, only with each other. Both of them allowed him to penetrate, but they were always engaged with one another in some type of way. Be it soul or saliva. They played their roles well, and in the end, the client left pleased and panting. The door closed behind them, and Ty fell asleep in Nicole's arms. The cocaine had Nicole still awake and alert. She stroked Ty's hair absentmindedly.

The next morning, Nicole had already gotten up and was in the shower when there was pounding at the door. It was Cloey. After knocking, she used the key to open the door. Ty was still passed out; Cloey hadn't expected Nicole, who was walking towel-wrapped around the room, to be asleep.

"I told y'all I would be here by 10. You have 15 minutes to be downstairs," Cloey grew aggravated because they were not ready. Her yelling woke Ty up from the sleep. Her head was pounding, and she could barely open her eyes. She had a headache that was intensified by the light.

"OK, we'll be downstairs, just chill out," Nicole yelled back. Cloey left the room.

"Please stop yelling," Ty said in a raspy voice.

"Just get up, she trippin'," Nicole was still intimidated by Cloey but not as much when she first met her.

After a half-hour, they left the hotel. Ty had a hangover and was barely able to walk on her own because she was so dizzy. In the back on the limousine, Cloey asked Ty, "Where am I taking you, missy?"

"She lives on campus," Nicole answered for her. The driver took Ty near the entrance of the dorms before she got out of the limo, Cloey handed her an envelope. It was her payment for the work she had done last night.

"'Preciate it," she said tersely. Then, softer, "Nicole, guess I'll talk to you later?"

"OK," Nicole responded. Ty closed the door, and Cloey asked Nicole where to drop her off.

She waited a moment before answering because she wanted to lie but really didn't need to this time. "Well, I technically live with Rachel-"

"What the hell? Not anymore, you don't." Cloey interrupted her before she could finish. "One of my buddies from back in the day leases condos on Ocean View. I know you can't afford it right now, but he owes me a favor. I'm sure he will let you live in one until he finds a permanent tenant." This was the first time Cloey had expressed any sincerity towards Nicole.

"Its levels to life and you and Rachel aren't the same."

"Well, can I at least get the rest of my clothes from Rachel's?" Nicole asked.

"Why not. Driver, go over to 87th off Hamilton."

On the way to Rachel's, Cloey called her guy to make sure Nicole could move in immediately. They arrived at Rachel's apartment building, and Cloey gave her the head nod to go ahead. As she walked upstairs, she wished Rachel was not home. Unfortunately, when she walked through the front door, she was sitting on the living room sofa, smoking a cigarette as if she had been waiting for her.

"Where you been, you didn't come home last night?" Rachel tried to sound casual.

Nicole did not answer, only headed to her room where her things were. She began to grab anything she could put her hands on. She tossed clothes, shoes, perfume, cosmetics, all of her belongings into hampers, storage bins, and suitcases. It did not matter; she was trying to get out of the apartment as quickly as possible. She could hear Rachel in the living room rambling about any and everything, but she barely cared. Before she knew it, Rachel was standing at her bedroom door.

"I see Cloey's limo downstairs," Rachel was livid. But she still had no idea what they had going on. At this point, she was just reaching, trying to get a reaction out of Nicole.

"Are y'all a thing now? Are you her bitch now?" Nicole, though infuriated, gave her nothing. She continued to pack her things wordlessly.

"You must be her hoe, turning tricks for your pimp."

Nicole reached in the hamper, grabbed a bottle of perfume, and threw it at Rachel before charging at her. Nicole was much smaller than Rachel, but because she caught Rachel off guard with her adrenaline pumping. She managed to back her into the hallway with her back against the wall. With one hand, she grabbed her throat, and with the other grabbed a handful of her synthetic hair, and slammed her onto the floor.

She stood over her and said, "I'm nobody's bitch and damn sure nobody's hoe." She hovered over her, staring her straight in the eyes and then walked out of the apartment. She didn't even take anything. She was furious. She got into the limo, slamming the door behind her.

"Where are your clothes?"

"Forget it. I'll buy more."

She shrugged. "Well, OK. The place is a go and is fully furnished so you won't have to worry about that. Just personal stuff, which it looks like you will buy more of."

Nicole was silent for the entire trip to the condo, thinking. They arrived at the manager's office, Cloey went inside and ten minutes later came back with the keys. She could tell Nicole was still upset about something but wasn't concerned enough to ask. The driver drove her to the building, the only one facing the ocean.

"Number 583." Cloey handed her the key and an envelope with her compensation. It was as if she was literally handing Nicole a new life, and that was the way it could have been perceived, but Nicole had a new agenda of her own.

Chapter 13

The previous night Jade had decided to return home and get back to Devin the next morning.

When morning came, she drove to his apartment and knocked on the door. Two minutes, then five. She kept knocking and knocking, but there was no answer. She assumed maybe he had already left for the day. Giving a long sigh, she turned and was walking back to her car to when she saw his car arrive.

She was excited yet nervous to see him. That was until he got out of the car, looking as if he had been up all night. He was moving slower than normal in a much-drained manner, wiping his face with his hand. She automatically assumed he had spent the night with another woman and was just getting back home.

"Where have you been?" Jade asked with an attitude.

"Look, I've had a long night, I don't have time for this," he added.

"Well, it's obvious you had a 'long night' and what you mean, 'you don't have time for this?" She took his words in and snapped back.

"This. OK. Jade, my mom is in the hospital, and I've been up all night."

Jade felt her heart drop and almost felt terrible until she remembered the last four words Nicole had said to her, "man is playing you."

"Yeah, right, you are just gonna tell me anything. You're nothing but a liar." She jabbed back. "I just came over here to tell you that I am going to Jamaica next week and probably moving to LA after graduation." Devin replied nonchalantly, "That's great, Jade. I'm happy for you! Congrats!"

That unexpected reaction made Jade very upset. She was at a loss of words. She walked past him, got in her car, and sped off back to her apartment. A million thoughts ran through her mind. Given the way he reacted, she was certain there was definitely another woman.

Later that night, Rachel went to her work as usual. She was working the floor with her usual clients; then, Tyreke walked in, searching around. Watching him sent her in a frenzy. She didn't know how to tell him that she and Nicole had an altercation, and Nicole moved out. She didn't know how he would react to the information. She had taken the advance, a couple of days had passed, and she had nothing new to tell him; at least nothing she thought could help him.

After her dance, she went over to where he was at the bar and braced herself to inform him about the fight they had, ready to bear his anger.

"Hey, what's been going on?" She asked, trying to break the ice and feel out his mood. He avoided her question and instead asked his own.

"How's Nicole? Where is she?" Rachel wasn't expecting him to be as blunt. All she could do was match the eagerness of his tone and be straightforward with him.

"Well, she moved out of my apartment. We kinda had a fight."

"So, did you get anything before she left?"

"I mean, not really, no." Rachel couldn't help feeling disappointed with herself. She let her head drop, then continued, "She didn't even say anything, she just came after me."

Tyreke was an emotional man, and so, forgetting his own concerns, he began to empathize with her. He patted her back and tried to say comforting words.

"I called her a bitch and a hoe and told her Cloey was her-," Rachel stopped mid-sentence, and her eyes grew wide. It all started to come together. Tyreke's hand stopped short of her back. He was confused, "Cloey was her what?" He asked, but Rachel didn't say a complete thought, only pieces of what her brain was analyzing.

"A hoe... well, there's her new job... can't tell you... uh, side hustle... It's complicated." She tried to piece it together.

"What are you saying, what does all of this mean?" Tyreke asked, desperate for meaning.

"That's why she came after me." Rachel was still thinking out loud to herself.

"Why did she come after you?" Rachel looked up at his anxious face. She had put it together but didn't want to tell Tyreke just yet. Not until she was very certain about it.

"Listen, Tyreke. If what I think is going on is really going on, I need to be 100% sure about it before I tell you... It's kind of... it's kinda bad."

Tyreke was disappointed because he thought she was about to tell him. He didn't respond immediately. But eventually, after giving it more thought, he asked, "How are you going to be 100% sure when you aren't even living together anymore? Let alone talking?"

She had not thought about that part, but she knew she would have to go above and beyond to find out. "Don't worry. I'll get the truth by any means necessary.

"Come to the club tonight, new gig on the table."

It was 3 P.M., and Nicole had just woken up by a text message from Cloey. She responded, "I'm there." She managed to get herself up and out on the balcony.

The view was so divine it took Nicole's breath away. She could not even take it all in a while standing, so she sat on the concrete floor grounding herself, and looked out at the ocean through the handrail bars. It was a beautiful sight to see.

Nicole lived near the ocean her entire life but had never taken the time to absorb its wonder and beauty. She felt like she was doing it for the first time in her life. She kept sitting there for a while, looking out at the beach and the water. She felt as if she was in a fairy tale until the handrail bars brought her back to reality. Because she was sitting and not standing, she felt like she was in a prison cell. In truth, she was in confinement by Cloey. She had changed her way of living, and Nicole knew the type of person Cloey was. She would hold that over her head. Nicole knew she could not continue to work with Cloey and allow her to do all the favors for her. Because it would eventually catch up with her, and things would only keep worsening.

So, she began to develop a way to get from under Cloey's control. First, she knew she would need money. She opened the envelope and counted $4,000 just as Cloey had promised. She estimated she would need about ten-thousand dollars to leave and start a new life in a new location altogether. She also figured it would take at least two to three more gigs to reach that amount.

"But where would I go?" She asked herself aloud. "Maybe Atlanta,? Nah, too close." She answered her own question. "Los Angeles?"

She meditated for a moment; her hair and face were rolling in the breeze. A smile began to grow on her lips, "LA, that's perfect," she said.

Nicole knew her and Jade's dispute wouldn't last very long because it never did. She compartmentalized in her mind that she would make up with Jade right before she left for Jamaica and seek her help to decide on the job.

She had a plan in progress, and the first step in accomplishing it would be to meet with Cloey for the particulars of the next gig. She got herself together and prepared to meet with Cloey later that afternoon.

When Nicole walked through the club to get to Cloey's office, she didn't get as much attention as she used to. No one paid attention to her anymore, now that they all knew she didn't want their attention. All except Rachel only glanced at her and moved their eyes past her.

Nicole had become so comfortable she didn't even knock on Cloey's door anymore. She walked right in. Cloey was on the phone, and as soon as Nicole entered the room, she placed her index finger over her lips, signaling her to be quiet. Nicole sat down as Cloey continued with her call.

"Uh-huh… OK…tomorrow evening. They will be there. OK. Goodbye, take care." Cloey hung up the phone." She cut the call before acknowledging Nicole. "Well, our next gig is set. Tomorrow at 7 P.M."

"Alright, what's the scene?" Nicole asked.

"This guy is a little less… physical. He just wants to watch two beautiful girls have sex," Cloey answered.

Nicole didn't mind. She was there just for business. "How much?"

"Well, this is a light job." Cloey began. "$1000 for everybody. You get that hot lesbian couple scene, and each of them gets a thousand, including you."

"OK, I will have the girls ready for pick up by 6, and I'll let you know their location by the morning."

Nicole had already stood up and was making her way to the door. She did not want to spend any unnecessary time around Cloey. Before she made it to the door, Cloey had already jumped out of her seat and, in an instant, was in front of her.

"Whoa, whoa, whoa, are you in a hurry?" She held the door just as Nicole was just about to turn.

"Nah, I'm just tired. And I have to make sure the girls will be available tomorrow." Nicole answered straight.

"That's understandable. The least you can do is let me make sure you make it back to that quarter-million dollar condo safely." She gave Nicole a subtle look as if to say she still is the boss.

Now Nicole was uncomfortable. She knew the type of person Cloey was and had foreseen her holding this favor too over her head. She had no other place to go, and as much as she didn't want to admit it, she needed Cloey. For now, at least.

Cloey put her arm around Nicole's neck, opened the door, and escorted her downstairs into the club. The sight of Cloey's arm around Nicole's neck grabbed the attention of every pair of eyes in the room.

The person it bothered most was Rachel. Watching the view and thinking about the two sent her mind in a frenzy. She felt betrayed and scattered. She was feeling more desperate than she would like to admit.

She thought to herself, "If they are together now, why didn't Nicole get mad at me when I said it? Or maybe she's trying to make me think they are together, so I don't think she's a hoe?"

Her mind raced and raced. Rachel was at her most vulnerable. She looked at the exit, thinking if she should break into Cloey's office. Again she looked, then aimed finally for the office and proceeded up the stairs. She crept up each step and constantly looked over her shoulder to ensure no one was watching or following her.

Once she reached the top of the staircase, she pulled a hairpin from her hair, expecting to have to pick the lock. To her surprise, the door was unlocked.

She hurried inside and eased the door shut behind her. She went directly to the desk. Papers were scattered everywhere, but nothing looked useful. She rummaged through Cloey's drawers and saw an untitled notebook. The only thing on the cover was a dollar sign. She flipped it open, and her jaw fell.

There was a list of names, and beside each name was a date, their fantasy, and a price. Rachel partially remembered the prices. They ranged from $20K to $50K. She kept flipping the pages and the breakdown of what each user was getting paid for each gig. It was in a pyramid. Cloey was at the top, making the most money. Right below her was Nicole, who only made about a thousand dollars more than the group titled, 'Others.'

Rachel didn't know exactly who the 'Others' were, but she had a decent guess about it. She closed the notebook and the drawer, then left the office. Luckily, no one had noticed Rachel. She rushed to the locker room, changed her clothes, and left the club. She had to call Tyreke twelve times before he finally answered.

"Meet me at 103rd and Cypress ASAP and bring the rest of the money." She hung up the phone and sat at a bus stop waiting for him to come. Thirty-five minutes later, Tyreke pulled up in his drop-top coupe. "Come on, get in," he yelled to her.

Once Rachel was inside the vehicle, she said, "Damn fool, do you have to be so flashy?" Tyreke looked confused. "We're supposed to be discreet, right? How are we gonna go unseen in a red convertible?" Rachel added. Tyreke sat frozen on the driver seat, feeling dumbfounded.

"Go to the carwash."

On the way to the car wash, Rachel was checking every vehicle that passed by because she did not want anyone to see her with Tyreke. Once they arrived, Tyreke parked the car and asked: "What's going on?" Before she jumped right into telling him, she had to warn him it was an ugly situation.

"What I'm going to tell you will disappoint you... A lot. So I want you to brace it."

"Just tell me, I can handle it."

She looked at him for a bit longer, then bluntly said, "Nicole is prostituting and setting up young girls to do it too."

Tyreke did take it well, but he was confused. "What do you mean, she's turning tricks for a couple of dollars. Doesn't she make more at the club dancing?"

"It's not the typical 'stand-on-the-corner, guy-takes-you-around-the-corner' prostitution." Rachel paused. "There's big money involved, that's why she kept it from me."

"How much money?"

"At least 20 grand."

He nodded. "So you're telling me, Nicole is sleeping with guys for 20 grand?"

"That's where it gets complicated. Cloey sets up the gigs. She gets the guys. Nicole finds the girls, and she has sex with the guys sometimes too."

Tyreke furrowed his brow. "How do you know this for sure?"

Rachel had an answer for every question. "I saw how they get paid, Cloey gets the most money, then Nicole, and finally the girls."

Tyreke sat there for a whole minute in disbelief, taking it all in, processing it. "OK, give me Cloey's number."

"Why?" Rachel asked, dubious. He pulled out an envelope from his jacket and showed her the cash inside.

"Number, please." She did not exactly want to give it, but she couldn't resist the money. Rachel gave him Cloey's number. He threw the envelope at her feet and said, "Now, get out of my car."

Chapter 14

"Good morning, beautiful." The text from Devin woke Jade up.

She didn't want to respond, but she was weak when it came to him. She didn't want to appear soft either, so she replied sarcastically. "So I'm beautiful now?"

Instead of responding through text, he called, and of course, she answered.

"Let's meet up later," he insisted.

"Why should I?" She was trying to play hard to get. Devin didn't have time for Jade's games. He knew her well enough by now.

"I will be at the diner across from the supermarket in two hours with or without you." He hung up, forcing Jade to make a decision. All the while, she knew she would meet with him, but she had wanted to give him a hard time for it. She got out of bed and prepared herself to meet with him later. Meanwhile, Nicole was ensuring things ran smoothly with the next gig. She called Tameka and Jessica and explained to them the terms and conditions of what would happen later that night. It would be similar to her and Ty's job. She explained to them that the man would be watching the girls as they would make love to each other, and each of them would get $1000 for it. She even stretched it and gave them tips.

"Just pretend like you two are the only people in the room. Imagine he is not even there. Never make eye contact with him and just focus on one another."

She informed them when to be ready and about how long the job would take. They both were all in. Immediately, after she hung up the phone, Nicole thought of Jade. She didn't mean what she said to her at that moment; it was merely out of spite towards Devin. She wanted to call Jade but could not make herself do it. Her pride always got in the way of her relationships; this she was aware of. She decided to delay her apology until the next day.

When Jade walked into the diner, Devin was already seated and eating. She took a seat across from him, "I guess you thought I wasn't going to come," she said, looking at his half-eaten plate of food. He didn't want to beat around the bush with Jade, so he swallowed his food and got right to the point.

"Look, Jade, I really care about you. I've never met a girl like you before. When we first met, you were different than the person you are turning into now."

Jade was taken back and only stared at him speechlessly, then looked here and there for some help. She was saved from responding by the waitress who had walked up to the table.

"Will you be dining with us today, ma'am?"

"I sure will, for starters, I will take an orange juice and toast and uh… Let's see." Jade was content with stalling.

"Jade," Devin took the menu from her, "Did you not hear what I just said?" Still not entirely prepared to respond, she now stalled with more fluff.

"Yes, I hear you, but it's just all words-"

Devin interrupted her, "Do I need to prove everything to you?"

He pulled out his cellphone and began to dial numbers. He put the phone on speaker and placed it on the table, "Grace Memorial, how may I help you?" Devin was calling his mother, who was still in the hospital. He kept the phone on speaker until he was connected to his mother's room, and Jade heard them talk on the phone. The conversation was brief. Once he hung up the phone, he said, "There, happy now?"

Still not wanting to surrender and give in to him, she replied, "OK, your mom is in the hospital, still doesn't justify where you were last night."

"You're unbelievable," Devin, pulled back in his chair, shocked.

Jade didn't feel anything about his mother's hospitalization due to the lack of bonding with either his or her own mother. Despite Jade's reaction, Devin still wanted her, and he wasn't going to give up easily. He was willing to go above and beyond to prove himself to her. He knew there was nothing he could tell Jade; he had to show her actions.

He stood up, placed two twenty-dollar bills on the table, kissed her forehead, and whispered, "I'm going to show you. You'll see." His forehead kiss still made her heart sink into her stomach and disperse as a million butterflies. She didn't expect Devin to get up and leave her as he did. She sat there dumbfounded, with a stomach full of butterflies trying to put the pieces back together.

Later that evening, Cloey called Nicole, "Hey, the girls are in the room as we speak. Since this is shorter than a normal gig, I will stay in the area so I can pay them and take them back home tonight." Cloey usually didn't call Nicole. She knew Cloey was trying to get too comfortable, and she would have to break ties sooner than later.

"Well that's cool, I will pick up my cut tomor-." Nicole couldn't finish her sentence before Cloey hung up to answer another call.

"Hi, I'm looking for Cloey," the voice on the other end said.

"This is Cloey, who am I speaking with?" she said gently. Even though she was rough with the girls in the club, Cloey knew how to be professional when the job required it of her.

"Uhmm, this is Anonymous."

It was apparent the voice hadn't planned out the conversation too well.

"How can I help you, Anonymous?"

"You can help me with the services you have been providing lately."

"I service lots of things; you have to be more specific." Cloey was trying to recognize the voice, but it was not familiar at all.

"I want your prettiest, most attractive girl." Cloey instantly thought of Nicole.

Being clever, the voice said, "But I have a few conditions. The girl must wear a masquerade mask. I want the set up to be Paris-themed. She has to dance for me in lingerie before sex."

"OK, that won't be a problem. I typically don't allow one girl for protection purposes. So, are you sure you don't want two girls?"

The voice took a deep sigh, "One girl for one hundred thousand dollars."

Cloey was instantly on the edge of her seat. Without any further hesitation, she replied. "Deal, next weekend."

The voice replied, "I will call you the night prior around this same time."

Before Cloey could close the deal, the voice had ended the call. She felt lost for words. She wanted to call Nicole and tell her right away, but she was on the job with Jessica and Tameka. She had to finish up that night. As she sat in the back seat of the limo, she had already divided the distribution in her head. She was planning to give Nicole only $20,000 of the promised $100,000, keeping the remaining for herself. She knew Nicole would jump at the opportunity because of the amount.

The next morning, Cloey was at Nicole's condo bright and early, banging on the door. Nicole thought it was the owner evicting her. She sleepily opened the door to find Cloey on her doorstep, as anxious as a teenage boy about to have sex for the first time. This sight woke her up. Nicole had no other choice but to invite her in as much as she didn't want to. Clinginess; this was the exact reason why Nicole knew she had to get away from Cloey.

Annoyed and frustrated, Nicole asked, "I know you aren't over here this early and this anxious to give me a lousy thousand dollars."

Reaching in her back pocket for her wallet, Cloey said, "Oh yea, about that," and handed Nicole a thousand dollars in fresh, crisp hundred-dollar bills. "Last night, I got a life-changing phone call for both of us."

"From who?" Nicole asked.

"So, check this out, we've done two gigs so far, and you've made what, $3500? How does 20 G's for one night sound like?" Nicole fell back on her seat on the sofa because she couldn't believe her ears.

"Come again?" she demanded, to make sure she heard correctly.

"20 Gs, one night, just you? This guy requested my prettiest, most attractive girl. No one else came to mind but you." Cloey thought she was telling Nicole she could make 20 grand in one night, but what she was actually telling her was that she was about to have enough money to leave the town for good.

"When is the job?"

Cloey smiled, "A week from now."

Knowing when the job was only built a timeline for Nicole. She needed to talk to Jade before her trip to Jamaica, and by the time Jade came back, she would do the gig and move to California with her. Nicole had zoned out while mentally making her dreams come true.

"Is that OK?" Cloey said as she left the condo. "Yes!"

Nicole immediately got dressed to go talk to Jade. It took her three buses and a quarter-mile walk to get to her apartment. She had never apologized to anyone about anything. This was the first time for Nicole. Her heart was pounding as she knocked on Jade's door. She knocked and knocked until she could finally hear her voice through the door, "What do you want?"

"Can you let me in, please?"

Jade was still upset with her, "Why should I?"

"Because I am your sister, duh?" Nicole tried to lighten the mood, but Jade was not taken by it.

Nicole took a deep breath, leaning against the door, "OK, I'm sorry, Jade. I really am."

Nicole pulled back as she sensed Jade start to unlock the door and twist the knob. Jade pushed the door open; Nicole walked over to the sofa and crashed on it.

"I think you were right about Devin." Nicole didn't say

anything; she wanted more words to come from Jade. "Nothing adds up with him anymore. He does a lot of talking, but it's just words."

By this time, Nicole had sat down as well. "He has me everywhere right now."

"What are you going to do?" Nicole managed to sneak in between Jade's sulking.

Surprisingly, Jade answered with a question. "I don't know. What would you do in my situation?"

Nicole was surprised by the question, but she knew she had to answer it with bias, so Jade would leave him and take the job in LA. She knew she had to be crafty with her word choice and use Jade's good intentions against herself.

"Well, it depends. If you want to be with Devin, you're going to stay with him regardless. But at the end of the day, you have to be satisfied with yourself. That's all that ultimately matters."

"What are you saying, exactly?" Jade asked.

"If you want to feel better, then even the score. If you can't swallow the pill of cheating, then leave and go to LA."

"You know I'm not the cheating type," Jade replied.

Nicole smirked, "I know."

"I leave for Jamaica the day after tomorrow, and I don't want to see him before because he will cloud my judgment."

"So, don't see him," Nicole replaced Jade's uncertainty. "Go pamper yourself. Get a Mani, Pedi. Go to the salon and the mall."

She reached in her purse and gave Jade a thousand dollars. Jade's face expression had a million questions.

"Don't think about it; just enjoy yourself. I will be here when you get back."

And Jade did just what her sister suggested.

Chapter 15

As Jade walked through the lobby of the airport dragging her luggage, she was amazed by the cultural differences. She approached a group of people standing near the exit. Most of them were holding signs. She glanced through the crowd to find her name. 'Jade Cartier,' it said. A woman was holding the sign.

She walked up to her and said, "Hi, my name is Jade."

The woman responded with a thick Jamaican accent, "Oh, welcome, Mrs. Cartier." Jade immediately corrected her, "I'm sorry, but it's Carter, and I am not married."

"Oh my, me apologies guh, so yuh luking fa island byow, eh?"

Jade could barely comprehend what she was saying, "Uh... No? Nothing like that."

The Jamaican woman responded, "Awh, she shyyy."

Jade just smiled back and didn't say anything else on the commute to the hotel. When they pulled up, Jade was greeted by a finely built local man, dressed in a black tuxedo. He opened her door and said in his own accent, "Welcome to Paradise Resorts."

Behind him stood a marvelously tall building. The concierge grabbed her suitcase from the shuttle bus and opened the door to the entrance of the hotel. In the center of the lobby was the largest water fountain she had ever seen. She automatically gravitated towards it.

The water shot up into the air, forcing Jade's eyes to follow it. The hotel had to have over 100 floors, and through the glass ceiling, one could see the beautiful Jamaican skies. Jade felt like she was truly in paradise.

"Ms. Cartier," the concierge was calling for her attention. "Ms. Cartier," he said once more.

"Yes, it's Carter." She finally snapped back to reality. "This place is so beautiful."

"Like a fairytale, I know," he said as he pointed her to the receptionist behind the counter.

"Jade Carter, with the athletic conference," she told the receptionist.

"We have been waiting for you, Ms. Carter," another woman beamed at her. She was the first person to pronounce her name correctly. "You are in room 1756; you will find the itinerary for the weekend in your room."

Jade walked towards the elevator, still in awe of how magnificent the hotel looked. Once she got to her room, she looked over the itinerary for the weekend.

The first event wasn't until later that evening in a private ballroom. It was a casual meet and greet. Although the event was informal, set in a relaxed environment, Jade was still nervous. Her social skills were subpar, and for this type of trip, she expected it to be strictly business. The prospect of gossiping and casual conversations dreaded her. She didn't want to think about the pressure of the upcoming night too much, so she took a nap.

Nicole had not left her apartment since she made amends with Jade. She did not want to risk running into anyone in public. The only thing she was focused on was finishing the last job and going to LA with a fresh start. Her days were consumed with the thoughts of Beverly Hills and the paparazzi. From time to time, she kept thinking of Tyreke and how she had treated him, then would quickly push that thought to the back of her mind. She thought of Jade and how she wished she was having the time of her life. She also thought of how she would have to manipulate Jade into moving to LA if she doesn't do it on her own.

Nicole knew Jade had a good thing going with Devin, and she didn't want to interfere with her sister's happiness. She also knew she had to leave town to have a new start in a new place, and that she wanted more than Jade's satisfaction.

"You must be Jade Carter from Tech University. I've heard so much about you."

A handsome man approached Jade at the bar in the lobby of the hotel. He had green eyes, golden-brown curls, and a smile as bright as a full moon on a dark night. Jade turned around, thinking it was someone she would recognize, but she did not. She sat there with a lost look on her face.

"Where are my manners? I'm Bill, here for the conference as well." He extended his hand to her.

Still confused as to how 'Bill' knew her, she just shook his hand and assumed he was another trainer from a different school trying to get the same position. Naturally going in her competitive mode, she acted polite yet distant. She didn't want to make friends with another candidate.

"Refill, ma'am?" The bartender asked Jade.

"Yes, and I will have a Jack and Coke," Bill answered before Jade could.

He stared at her, holding a perfect smile as the bartender prepared their drinks. She swiveled the chair, turning her back to him and mumbled, "So this is what people do now? Just buy strangers drinks."

"Actually I don't buy 'people' drinks. I bought one drink for a beautiful, intelligent young woman who I would like to get to know better."

Jade turned around to look him in his eyes. She tried her best not to blush and keep a straight face, but she couldn't hide it any longer. "Hmm," she said and checked him out. He was built square and muscular and had a brilliant fashion sense. Just as she began to smirk, Bill said, "And of course the lady would have to already been drinking... at a bar might I add."

Jade burst into laughter, which made Bill laugh. She immediately straightened up as the bartender brought out their drinks.

"You're not funny, ya know?"

"Well, comedy was never my strong suit, which is why I got into sports medicine because I knew I couldn't be a brain surgeon."

Now giggling, Jade asked, "Who are you again?"

"I'm Bill, remember? Doesn't seem like you'd make a very good brain surgeon either with that memory."

She laughed again and blushed, not even noticing people had started to fill the room.

She conversed with Bill some more. "Excuse me, I have to use the ladies' room," she eventually said.

Jade didn't realize how much she drank until she stood up and began to walk. She was already coming up with excuses to tell Bill why she would have to cut the night short and get back to her room. She couldn't be this intoxicated before such a handsome man. She talked to herself in the stalls, struggling for excuses until something sounded believable.

"My sister called, and my cat died. Nah, that doesn't sound reasonable. My sister called, and my grandma died,' she paused. "Girl, your grandmother is already dead," she spoke frustrated.

A voice yelled from the stalls, "Just tell him the truth, if he really likes you, he'll understand."

Now slightly embarrassed, Jade just repeated the voice as if it was her idea.

"You know I will tell him the truth, and if he's a stand-up guy, he'll be cool...yeah, that sounds good."

She left the bathroom, ready to tell Bill she was calling it a night and she would see him tomorrow. As Jade approached Bill, he was laughing and talking with a group of people.

"Excuse me, Bill. I just want to tell you it was great meeting you, but-," Jade was interrupted by someone on the microphone.

"Ladies and gentlemen, thank you all for coming to this lovely seminar. We have worked so diligently to put together. But without any further ado, I would like to introduce you to the man responsible for this event. Please help me welcome the best athletic trainer in the world, the man who has taught me everything I know, and the man you all are inspiring to become: Dr. William Doucet!"

"Hold that thought, sweetheart, the people are requesting me." Bill beamed at her charmingly.

Jade was beside herself with shock. The entire time she thought she was entertaining just another trainer from a different school, but the whole time she was speaking with Dr. Doucet. The Doctor Doucet.

She imagined he would be an older gentleman due to his accolades in the classroom and in the field. She was looking forward to meeting him the next day, once the seminar would begin but not in the meet and greet. Now, she was more embarrassed that she didn't pick up on 'Bill,' when he introduced himself. She also thought she lost her chance of being selected since Dr. Doucet saw her outside of a professional environment.

He spoke to the crowd for about 15 minutes, and Jade didn't listen to a word he said. She was still in disbelief. She asked the bartender for water to try and sober up before Bill finished his speech. She had a strong urge to go up to her room and pretend the night ever happened. She was trying to remember portions of their conversation she had said to try and reconcile the conversation and continue on a better path. She thought it was possible, now that she knew exactly who she was talking to. The crowd laughed and chuckled at Dr. Doucet's jokes, he was charismatic, and his attractive features made him more likable.

He ended his speech with a joke, "So remember, if you ever want to use me as a reference, never say, William or Dr. Doucet, always, always say 'Bill.'"

Jade felt worthless. She wanted to make a run for the door while she still had a chance, but she couldn't move. Bill flashed his smile and shook hands as he made his way through the crowd. The opportunity to leave was slowly fading with every step he took towards her. He looked up and made eye contact, and now she couldn't leave. She dropped her head and turned her back to face the bar.

"Don't be shy," Bill said as he placed his hand on her shoulder.

Jade slowly turned her barstool to face him. He could tell she was blushing even through her dark hue.

"I'm so sorry I didn't recognize you," she began. "You must think I'm a complete fool that I didn't even know who you were. I mean, I did… I mean, I do… like who doesn't know who Dr. William Doucet is."

She rambled on, and he smiled as she tried to explain herself.

"Sweetie, don't worry about it," he tried to reassure her, but she didn't hear him.

"Again, I'm sorry. I'll see you tomorrow at the conference." She grabbed her clutch from the counter and proceeded towards the door.

"Wait," he tried to grab her hand, but she yanked away from him. She stormed out of the exit door, which led to the beach. She couldn't walk through the lobby because she couldn't face running into someone. She held her head down and dug her feet into the soft, white sand.

She walked towards the water, close enough for the water to cover her feet before it retreated back to the roaring ocean, over and over again.

She stood on the sand and talked to the sea for a half-hour, telling the powerful waves that she hoped she didn't mess up a once in a lifetime opportunity. Jade turned around now carrying her shoes and clutch, and Bill was there, elegant and robust in the blowing wind. His eyes sparkled as the moonlight reflected in them. She tried to walk past him, but he stopped her and put his coat around her shoulders. They stood face to face; she was just as tall as him. He looked into her dark brown eyes, and she allowed herself to be seduced by the reflection of the moon in his. Then suddenly, shaking it away, she took the coat from around her, handed it to him, and said, "Goodnight, Dr. Doucet."

He smirked just enough so his cheek formed a dimple.

"Can't wait to see you tomorrow, Ms. Carter."

Bill stood alone in the sand as Jade walked away. On the way back to her room, she thought about Devin. She wondered what he was doing? Where he was? How his mom was doing? An overwhelming feeling of regret overcame her. She immediately concluded that he had already moved on from her, and she should do the same.

Her process of moving on was always along the lines of accomplishing another goal. She chuckled to herself as she thought that is the reason why she has been so successful with her educational career. Every time someone would hurt her, she would suppress the thought by drowning herself in work. She showered and prepared herself for bed and contemplated how she would begin to move on from Devin with impressing the committee and earning a position in Los Angeles. Despite being severely embarrassed, Jade was ending her night on a positive note. Just as she began to doze off, she was startled by a knock at her door. Initially, it frightened her because she was certain she put the do not disturb sign on the knob.

"Who is it?" She could hear the fear in her own voice as she waited for a response she never received. She looked through the peephole, and it was Bill. She was instantly relieved but anxious, too. Why he was at her door?

She opened the door just enough so he could see that it was her. Pretending to be half asleep, she said, "Why are you here?" Again, Bill did not respond. He pushed the door open enough so that he could enter. "What are you doing?" Jade asked. "I want you," Bill replied, looking at her intensely in the eyes.

Pushing the door open, he wrapped his arms around her waist and walked Jade to the bed. She complied. She did not stop him. She realized that she wanted him just as much as he wanted her. The thought of a man like him seeing her in a beautiful light made her feel special. She kissed him passionately and grabbed a handful of his golden curls. As he lay her body on the bed, situating himself on top of her, she thought about a nature trip she took her senior year in high school. He went down on her, and she, moaning, remembered walking across a canopy bridge in search of the rainbow waterfall deep into the forest.

Jade was running with her deductible juices, simultaneously remembering hearing the waterfall before she found it in the woods. Bill began to finger her while he smothered his face between her legs. It made her wild. The closer she walked to the waterfall, the closer she got to the climax. As her memory served her the vision of being just around a tree away from the waterfall, she whispered, "I'm about to cum."

After many hours of passion and pleasure, both Bill and Jade fell asleep in each other's arms. The next morning Jade rolled over to feel for Bill, but she found the space empty. She sat up and looked around. There was no sign of him. She returned under the covers thinking how sultry and sizzling had been. She saw multi-colored with back to back orgasms. She found it unbelievable to wrap her head around the idea that she had sex with Dr. Doucet. That she pleased him and he pleased her. She wondered how things would be between them now when they meet for competition? Will that affect her performance today?

She pulled the comforter from over her head… and was shell-shocked to find Devin in her room. He had not been there a few minutes ago, she thought. Or had she been too sleepy to notice? She was out of her senses. Her boyfriend had flown all the way to Jamaica to surprise her. He wanted to cheer for her from the crowds and back her up. This morning, however, his face showed no sign of excitement. It was blank, and he was standing at the foot of the bed with his arms folded. He had been waiting for her to awake

"How did you sleep?" Devin asked with a dark look in his eyes.

Jade searched for the right words to respond. Her mind was in a tornado now. Did he know for certain about her infidelity? Had he seen Dr. Doucet? For how long had he been in the room? Guilt and confusion raced in her as quickly as the blood in her veins. Devin could read her like an open book and tell she was bewildered and embarrassed. Before she could fabricate a story, he interrupted. "I saw your "new thing" leave out this morning. Must say that's one good catch. Good for you, girl."

"Devin, let me explai-," Jade felt a sob stick in her throat.

"There's nothing to explain," he started again. "You accused me of cheating, and all the while, it was you who couldn't be trusted. You don't have to worry about seeing me again."

Chapter 16

"Cloey speaking," she answered casually.

"Yes, hi, uhmm… this is Anonymous."

"Oh, hey!" Cloey sat up straight. "Are you ready to play out your fantasy in just a short few hours?"

"Yea, yea… You don't have to pitch a sell to me. I'm in already." On the other end, he seemed to be lighting a cigarette. "You tell me, is that girl ready?"

Tyreke was out of character, pretending to be firm and hard. Sensing the level of seriousness, Cloey switched from salesperson to boss immediately.

"You got my money?"

"A messenger will drop off an envelope with $50,000 to your club at noon."

"And the other half?"

"It'll be there tomorrow morning at 9 a.m."

"Alright then, let's do business."

She hung up the phone and excitedly called Nicole.

"Good morning, baby girl!"

Nicole was half asleep when she answered the phone. "Hey, Cloey."

"Today is the big day, wake up. I'm sending a car to get you in an hour."

"Wait. Why?" Nicole's raspy voice showed her grumpiness.

"I just want to get your day started the right way. Let's have breakfast." My day, she recalled. Yes, it was her day, indeed. Nicole really wasn't up for breakfast with Nicole, but she was hungry.

"Alright. Alright. Alright. I'm getting up now."

Although Nicole would have rather stay in bed a couple of hours longer, she forced herself to go ahead and kickstart her day. She felt good about the day and her life to come feeling as if things were really going to look optimistic hereon. She thought about what Cloey said, "Today is the big day."

But who could have told her what challenges and perils awaited her?

It was the day that would provide the opportunity for her to change her life forever. A new start, a fresh start, all that would begin with $20,000, she thought. Nicole focused on the night that was ahead of her. She planned about how she would wear her hair, what fragrance she would use, how she would seduce him, and foreplay with the client or how he would foreplay with her. The ultimate goal was the money, which was also the motivator. She thought it would also be the catalyst for her performance. Her eyes glinted at the thought.

Two hours later, Cloey's car picked Nicole up from her luxorious condo. She didn't expect Cloey to be there, let alone holding her door like the driver always did. Once inside, Cloey started complimenting Nicole. Her praises became overwhelming and obnoxious at one point.

"That's a nice perfume you're wearing, what's it called," Cloey asked. Nicole replied, pulling a face, "Chanel. I've only worn it every single day since you've known me."

"Well, today is special," Cloey snapped back in defense. Nicole rolled her eyes and looked out the window without thinking much about it. She had planned for this to be the last day she ever saw Cloey.

The car took them to Malone's, a fancy café where all the wealthy housewives had their weekly gossip over brunch. The waitress seated them and brought out bottomless mimosas. Cloey continued to patronize Nicole with her irritating remarks. "Has your hair always been that long?" Nicole only gave her a cold stare. "I guess I never noticed." Cloey felt Nicole's agitation, so she shifted the conversation. "Sooo, what are you going to do with all that money?" She saw the glint return in Nicole's eyes. Now Cloey was speaking her language.

"I'm probably gonna go somewhere..." she said and paused right away.

"Go where?" asked Cloey.

Nicole knew she said too much already. She was definitely planning to leave town and follow Jade to California. But she knew if Cloey found out, she would talk her out of it, especially since they are new profound business partners.

"I don't know," Nicole said, feigning uncertainty. "I really haven't given it much thought."

"Well, wherever you go, don't stay long 'cause we have a lot of money to make together," Cloey added as she sipped on her third mimosa.

The look of conceit on her face made Nicole wary. Her intuition gave her a bad feeling. When her gut made her feel this dubious, something usually turned out bad. She didn't want to believe it this time because there was too much at stake, so she ignored it.

"Do you want to go back to the condo to get some rest before your big night?" Cloey asked. They were both full on an All-American breakfast and loaded off mimosas.

"Nah, I'll catch a cab. I know you have other business to tend to."

"Well, at least let me give you cab fare and wait with you until it comes."

Feeling surprised but letting it go with a shrug, Nicole agreed to Cloey's offer.

"Take me to Palmetto Estates," Nicole told the cabby. She was going to Jade's apartment to leave a note on her door she had written last night. She knew that in order to get to Jade, she would have to pull at her heartstrings. Her sister liked simple yet meaningful gestures. Her hand-written letter would be perfect; she knew it. And so she went and slipped the note under the door, so it would be the first thing Jade saw when she returned home.

As she was leaving the apartment, she ran into Rachel at the staircase. Both of them were startled. "I've been looking everywhere for you," Rachel was panting.

"Why?" Nicole felt disgusted, just looking at her.

"I may have done something bad." Now she had Nicole's full attention. "I know what business you have with Cloey." Rachel spat out in one breath. Nicole's eyes grew to the size of golfballs. "And I met Tyreke…" she added meekly. And that was the last straw. Nicole let her anger take over and struck Rachel across the face.

"How dare you? Stay out of my business, bitch!" Nicole screamed. She was infuriated to the point that she didn't even stay to hear what else Rachel had to say.

She called a cab to go back to her place, but not before stopping by the liquor store first. After chugging down an entire bottle of Vodka, Nicole realized she was two hours away from her life-changing appointment. She freshened up once more before calling for Cloey's car and snorting a hasty line of cocaine. She was excited but anxious too. She wanted the job to be over already. She dreamt of endless beaches and palm trees, but her reveries were interrupted by her ringing phone. Her ride was downstairs.

Fortunately for Nicole, Cloey hadn't come along for the ride. She only sent a voice message through the driver. "Here is the key to the room; everything you need is already there. I will come back for you in the morning with your twenty grand." Nicole was partially listening and partially focused on getting through the night for her reward the next morning. Just then, her phone rang. It was Rachel; she declined the call. She received a text immediately thereafter, "Please call me. I really need to talk to you." She ignored that as well. "Just one more night," she told herself. "Just this one bloody, final night."

The driver pulled up to the Ritz Carlton Hotel. This was shocking to Nicole because the clientele Cloey dealt with usually wanted to keep a low profile because a lot of them were married men. Hotels of this status would increase the likelihood of them running into a colleague, Nicole thought. As quickly as she had thought about the risk, she pushed it to the back of her mind just as swiftly. She tried to remain focused on the task at hand. "Cloey wanted me to give you some extra motivation for such an important job," the driver surprised her as he handed Nicole two pills that looked more like candy than drugs. Nicole shot him a dirty look as she reached out her arm to get the pills. He smirked and also handed her a key card, 'room 1159'. "Enjoy your night," he told her. She snatched the key card and hurried out of the car. She ingested the pills in the elevator on the way to the room.

Inside the room, she found a note with written instructions. "Change into the lingerie on the bed, and don't forget the mask." Nicole followed the directions and waited impatiently. Five minutes, ten, fifteen, and then twenty minutes passed away. On the twenty-first minute, Tyreke opened the door just wide enough so the sound of his voice could travel through. "Are you ready?" His voice startled Nicole. She thought it sounded familiar, but she wasn't sure. She just might have been tripping on the Ecstacy and Cocaine combination. "Yes, I'm ready."

Tyreke was wearing an all-black t-shirt and pajama pants. His face was covered up with a masquerade mask so she couldn't recognize him. He eased into the room and went directly to the closet. Nicole's eyes followed, confused. He pulled restraining straps from a dark-colored duffel bag. Nicole felt a little uneasy. "This wasn't a part of the agreement," she blurted out. Tyreke put his index finger over his lips, "shhh."

He restrained each of her legs first. Then he kissed her smooth, confined legs until he reached her black, silk-laced panties. Her arms reflexively clutched his shoulders, and so Tyreke went back to the bag and pulled out two more restraints and tied up each of her arms. Nicole tried not to look too nervous and avoided looking at the man. He was a complete stranger, but there was something familiar about his aura. Once again, as she had been doing it all day, she pushed the thought away. She just wanted him to do his business and the night to be over.

She lay bound and spread-eagled in the middle of the bed. Tyreke found her exquisite and felt a hardening in his pants. He lowered over her slowly until his head was pillowed on her breasts. He snaked his arms underneath her and wrapped them around her waist. Nicole felt his bulge rest and grind ever so softly against her panties. She lost her breath.

"Why, Nicole?" Tyreke's voice came out muffled into her breasts.

"Why what?" She replied, her breath still hitched.

"Why do you have to do this?" He continued and gave her a kiss on her breast with every clause he spoke. "I could've given you the life you want, the life you deserve."

Nicole was high, aroused, and confused at the same time. Tyreke pulled himself away and stood at the foot of the bed. She craned her neck up to look at him. "I've watched you every day, you know. I can't sleep at night because you're always on my mind. I can barely eat. Look how thin I'm getting, look," Tyreke kept on confessing his obsession.

At first, Nicole assumed he was just a stalker. But the more he talked, the more Nicole's eyes started to bulge. She figured out it was him. "You're doing this for money, right? You could have come to me… I have plenty. I would have showered it upon you," he spoke like a child.

"Tyreke! That's you, Tyreke?" Nicole snapped.

He removed the mask, revealing himself. "Girl, I love you. We could have been perfect together. Why didn't you wanna be with me?" His voice quavered and, to Nicole's shock, a tear rolled down his face. He kept on pouring his heart out to her.

Nicole was at once flustered and furious. Her mind raced with a million thoughts per minute. *Did Cloey set me up? Was this the reason she had been so nice to me? How did I not see this coming? Have I been too blinded by the thought of freedom?*

"I gave that madam of yours a hundred grand to get you alone, and now you have nothing to say?" Tyreke cocked his head to one side, breaking Nicole's contemplation.

"Wait. What?" Now she was really pissed. He had answered half of her questions, and she wanted to kill Cloey. But she knew she couldn't show any anger. She soon realized that in order to get out of her shackles, she would have to play nice. She had to make Tyreke feel that she would be with him. It was difficult to do, but she softened her expressions.

"Baby, I'm so sorry I did you wrong. Give me a chance to make it right… Take these restraints off me, come on, and we can talk about it." Their eyes connected. He saw the moisture in her eyes and mistook it for redemption. He believed her, and his lips stretched to a smile. "Please, baby, they are hurting me," Nicole pleaded. Tyreke rushed over to one side of the bed. He grabbed her face and kissed her passionately. There was fire and feeling in his kiss, and a touch of madness; madness for her. She kissed him back even though she did not want to. Every moment he invaded her mouth, something boiled inside her, and she hated him more and more.

She hated him for taking advantage of her; she hated him for Cloey. She hated him for the feelings she always suppressed about her sister. And finally, she hated him for making her last night so difficult. And as he was patiently unfastening the restraint on one of her arms, all of this hate rose up in her like bile. As soon as her arm was free, her first reaction was to slap him.

The slap at once took Tyreke by surprise and angered him. He struck her face back and strapped down her only free limb down. She could see the mix of betrayal and fury in his eyes, but she didn't care. Nicole was in an angry trance of her own. She spat on his face and threatened to go to law enforcement as soon as she got free. She simultaneously pulled at each restraint, hoping she could wiggle herself free.

She was unsuccessful, and like that, the fight in her was sinking slowly and slowly. Tyreke could see the alarm on her face now. Three of her limbs were still tied up, and she was helpless to his mercy again. Tyreke allowed himself to relax. He let go of her hand and stood away from the bed just to mock her helpless efforts. She tried to unstrap herself, but the knots he had made were sailor-level complex.

She resorted to screaming as loud as she could, and to her despair, he joined in by echoing her cries for help with louder screams. She figured it out before he gave a wicked smile and said, "Soundproof walls sweetheart." The next part was surprising for her when he said, "Plus, I reserved both rooms on each side; you know, just to be on the safe side." He laughed at his own humor, and Nicole felt like she was in vertigo, all out of options.

"Please, Tyreke, I will do anything you want me to." But the time for that was gone. The tears that streamed down her cheeks evidenced that.

"You lost that chance when you hit me, you dumb bitch."

"But what now? What are you going to do to me?"

"What I should have done from the beginning." The sinister look in his eyes horrified her.

He climbed on top of her and started to kiss and suckling her breasts and neck.

"What are you doing? No! Stop!" She begged him with closed eyes.

He only continued to moan as he did until his penis was fully erect. In one swift motion, he pulled his pants and boxers down. He pulled her panties to the side and penetrated her with a single thrust.

Nicole couldn't help the scream that left her throat. She sobbed with every thrust screaming, "Tyreke, please stop. Please!" She continued to plead with him, feeling weaker and weaker as his huge shaft split her belly in half.

He grunted hysterically as he shoved his hips harder and faster into her like a piston. She felt delirious and could not form any intelligible words. Tyreke covered her mouth with his hand and gave her a hickey on her neck as he raped her.

The sweat from his forehead dripped onto her face, and he continued violating her body until his body stilled, and he climaxed inside her. She didn't look at his face and sealed her lips shut to reveal no emotion. Something shifted in her, and she felt her jaw stiffen. He rolled over onto his back, panting hard, and lay his head on her shoulder. She was staring up at the ceiling next to him, her anger and hate rising up again.

"Now you're stuck with me forever," he said, coming maliciously close to her face.

Nicole, to his utter shock, rather than being devastated, scoffed at him. "Haven't you ever heard of abortions, genius?" He rolled back over on top of her, now straddling her.

"You'd do that to me?" He was cowering at her, something very vicious and vile taking over him. Nicole saw red right then, but couldn't understand that he was going farther away from his senses.

"Why don't you understand, I---." Before she could complete, both of Tyreke's hands were around her throat. Her eyes widened, and the veins in her neck bulged broader, complementing the veins popping in his hands and forearms. She wiggled and squirmed under him, contorting her body this way and that. It only made his grip tighter. She tried to speak, but her voice came out in gasps. He was hysterically fuming at the mouth, drooling on top of what was her pristine flesh just twenty minutes ago. Her eyes were blinking rapidly, legs were wringing uncontrollably until slowly and slowly, the motions descended, and within a minute of struggling, all movement escaped her body.

Tyreke's chokehold had not seized until a good ten more seconds after she died. When his hysteria evaporated, Tyreke jolted back, delirious. He neared her again, shook her, slapped her, shook her again, but no sign of life responded. It settled in him for certain then. His hands were on his head, and his tears were falling on the marble floor.

"Oh, God. What have I done?"

Chapter 17

Two days after the event, Jade was back at her apartment, still exhausted down to her bone and soul. The moment she unlocked the door, she found a letter on the floor. She bent and picked it up and immediately recognized Nicole's handwriting.

Jade,

I know we don't always see eye to eye, and that's mostly because of me. I'm... a nutcase, I admit. I don't really know how to say this because I'm not good with words like you. But Ima try the best way I know to express myself. I think you are perfect. Perfect in every way, with your flaws even. I always envied how you are always looking out for yourself, and I can't seem to do anything right by myself. I have hated myself for not being as good as you, no matter how hard I tried. But lately, I have been wanting to make things right. I hope you understand where I'm coming from...

She immediately called Nicole. She could hardly wait to talk to her.

www.ingramcontent.com/pod-product-compliance
Lightning Source LLC
Chambersburg PA
CBHW050416260626
47156CB00003B/1032